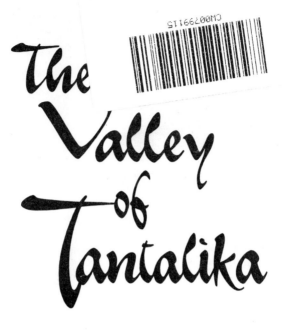

The Valley of Tantalika

RICHARD RAYNER

Illustrated by
ELEANORA ALEXANDER

Published by
BAOBAB BOOKS
HARARE

First published in 1980 by
Books of Zimbabwe Publishing Co. (Pvt.) Ltd.
Also published in 1984 by
MacDonald Purnell, Johannesburg

Published by Baobab Books,
a division of Academic Books (Pvt.) Ltd.,
P.O. Box 567, Harare. 1990

Reprinted 1995

ISBN 0 908311 28 1

Printed by Mazongororo Paper Converters (Pvt.) Ltd.,
Harare, Zimbabwe.

To

Shirley-Anne and Deborah,
who enjoyed the first pages
and asked me to write more.

Foreword

This story, which Richard Rayner relates with tenderness, with compassion and with deep understanding of the wild animal world, brings a touch of bush magic to an event in Zimbabwe's history which was fraught with hardship and havoc.

Only someone as familiar as the author with the inhabitants of the Zambezi valley and all it contains could persuade the reader into a realm of fantasy with such conviction. For me, after the first reading, Tantalika, the wise otter, became someone I felt I knew intimately and regretted leaving at the end of the last page. It does not, in any way, seem strange that he possesses the gift of extra-sensory perception or the ability to communicate with animals of a different kind. What, after all, do we know of this fascinating field which is, as yet, shrouded in mystery, both in the human and animal spheres?

This enchanting, absorbing book is for everyone, anywhere, in and out of Africa. It will give you pause to wonder at the similarity between the Valley dwellers and yourself; your griefs and joys, your doubts, your longing for a new era in a better world devoid of cruelty and strife, when the godkin Fura-Uswa will never again have cause to be angry with the two-legged Zimikile.

SUE HART.

White River,
South Africa,
May 1980.

About the Author

Richard Rayner has spent a lifetime writing, producing and editing documentary films in Zimbabwe and elsewhere. His published work includes many short stories and two other full-length books: *Who Cares? – Chipangali* (1977) and *Tsoko: The Story of a Vervet Monkey,* published by Baobab Books (1990). His story for children, *Umboko and the Hamerkop,* was also published by Baobab Books (1988).

Introduction

EARLY on the morning of the third of December, 1958, an event occurred in Southern Africa which, at the drop of a man's hand, outdated all the maps hitherto drawn of Northern and Southern Rhodesia, as the countries of Zambia and Zimbabwe were then known.

From the instant when the signal was given to close the last gaps in the Kariba dam wall, the waters which had flowed for at least half a million years from the gorges below the Victoria Falls to the gorge at Kariba were held captive; 175 miles of the Zambezi river were stilled, broadening in a few years into the largest man-made lake in the world, at that time.

For years men had toiled to complete this achievement, from when, in the early days, small teams of specialists battled through the dense, sometimes impenetrable bush. Surveyors mapped the lie of the land; geologists and seismologists sought faults in the river bed and the rock buttresses where the dam was to be built; and all the hundreds of relevant details were logged and collated, then passed on to the planners, the architects, the engineers and the construction teams. The end result, in that last month of 1958, was a concrete arch wall, 420 feet high, nearly 2 000 feet across, with all the paraphernalia of underground turbines, control equipment, overhead cables and switching stations to provide the power needs of a new, developing nation, the Federation of Rhodesia and Nyasaland.

Never before, on the African continent, had any work of man caused such a manipulation of a large, wild and natural area, influencing countless millions of living creatures, from the microscopic river plankton to the largest land mammal on earth, the elephant; from the tiniest plant cell to the huge baobab tree which can live for a thousand years or more. For them and the primitive tribespeople whose homes, for generations, had been close to the river, it all began when squads of men from far away came into the Zambezi valley.

Their purpose was to clear vast tracts of forest land, so that the future lake could become a great fishing ground, where the submerged branches of drowned trees would not foul the nets. They came to eradicate the tsetse fly from areas where the river dwellers would resettle, and because the fly feeds off the infected blood of many animal species, they also had to be destroyed.

When the dam was closed, there were the first, courageous efforts of a pitifully small, dedicated band of men who risked their lives daily to save animals drowning in the flood, starving on new-formed islands, or marooned in trees which were being engulfed by the rapidly rising waters. This inspired, selfless exercise captured the imagination of people all over the world, and those who cared for the welfare and preservation of this wild kingdom donated in cash and kind their help, which poured into Southern Rhodesia. The company of rescuers increased its numbers, and from operating with two decrepit launches, with only the barest necessities, they became better equipped, and between 1958 and 1964 over 7 000 animals, countless birds, reptiles and even insects had been saved from the flood.

In telling the story of these stirring events, seeing them through the eyes and minds of some of the animals who had no choice but to submit to them, I have been aware that the line drawn between fact and fiction can be made so thin that it may become almost invisible. To avoid any misunderstandings, therefore, especially among the young, I must make this quite clear: where my animal and bird characters become 'anthropomorphised', that is, attributing to them human speech, emotions, and sometimes exaggerated powers of reasoning or physical strength, the reader enters into the world of fantasy — and I make no apologies for that because the Zambezi valley itself is, and always has been, a place for myth and magic.

Characters of the Valley

All the animal characters in this story were of a specific area in Africa, a part of the Zambezi valley, once thinly populated by the Batonka tribes. It therefore seemed appropriate to base their names on the Tonga language of these people.

The Pambuka Impalas

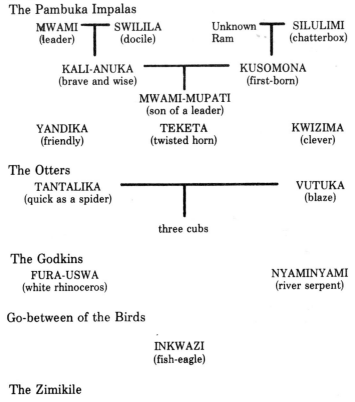

| MWAMI (leader) | SWILILA (docile) | | Unknown Ram | SILULIMI (chatterbox) |

KALI-ANUKA (brave and wise) — KUSOMONA (first-born)

MWAMI-MUPATI (son of a leader)

YANDIKA (friendly)　　　TEKETA (twisted horn)　　　KWIZIMA (clever)

The Otters

TANTALIKA (quick as a spider)　　　　　　　VUTUKA (blaze)

three cubs

The Godkins

FURA-USWA (white rhinoceros)　　　　NYAMINYAMI (river serpent)

Go-between of the Birds

INKWAZI (fish-eagle)

The Zimikile

IJONGOJONGO (the tall, thin man — Ndebele language)

Glossary

The following list of words and phrases used in the text are close translations from the Tonga language. They have been taken from English-Tonga dictionaries published some fifty years ago, kindly loaned by the Department of African Languages at the University of Zimbabwe.

inguluzi	tsetse fly
Ma-buyu	place of the baobab trees
mawe	mother
mulombe	a young male
Pambuka	aloofness
Zimikile	upright; standing on two legs

"ee!"	"yes!" or "hey there!"
"ka sike"	"farewell" (to the one departing)
"ko caala"	"farewell" (to the one remaining)
"nduwe ni?"	"who are you?"
"wa buka?"	"how are you?"

Months of the Year

Maziba	January
Kulumi	February
Muyobo	March
Kangala	April
Kanini	May
Gandapati	June (the coldest month)
Wasinkula	July (the falling of the leaves)
Bimbe	August
Tundwa	September (month of the new leaves)
Kavumbi	October (the hottest month)
Ikando	November
Nalupale	December (month of the early rains)

1

ALL along the central Zambezi valley, from the gorges east of the Victoria Falls to where the river twisted abruptly north from Kariba, over 150 miles away, an early summer storm was raging thunderously across the hills and escarpments, the sheets of rain washing away the deep-down topsoil, dust-dry from the winter months, soaking the forest trees down to their roots.

Far away, south-west of Kariba and quite close to the river bank, the lightning slashed and cracked over the mopane trees growing thickly on a low rise, where an impala doe sought privacy from the rest of the herd among the dense riverine bush and tall grasses. It was the same birth-site she had used before, where she felt safest from predators and the unwelcome attentions of young, curious males.

Swilila, the docile one, was no youngster. By human standards she was middle-aged, and had produced her first-born when she had been two years old, her second and third at yearly intervals thereafter. None had survived for long. The first had been taken by wild dogs, the second snatched from her by a tawny eagle, and the last had been carried away by floodwaters sweeping along the river early in the year.

She lay down for a while, head raised, ears stretched back, and groomed herself briefly. Then, shifting uncomfortably, she got up and wandered about, careful to keep out of sight, her hind legs slightly straddled, until she collapsed into a clump of grass, bleached white by the sun. For a long time she lay, straining, helping the new life struggling within her to release itself from the darkness in which it had grown for seven months. She tried to rise again, but fell back and lay on her side, with hind legs backward-splayed.

When the little impala came, front hooves first, struggling and sliding on to the wet grass, an explosive shaft of lightning flared to the fork of a nearby tree, splitting the branches. One fell, its foliage brushing gently against Swilila's flank — a comforting, reassuring caress.

It was at that moment she knew, with animal certainty, that this one would be different, that he would not only survive to maturity but would, in some way, make his mark in the small herd she had run with since her own birth. She would see him grow, unlike her others, into a fine impala ram, braver and wiser than any other — even his father Mwami, the leader of the herd — in this small corner of the Great Valley which would be his world. Because she knew he would be brave and wise, she named him Kali-Anuka.

The storm, which had played its rumbustious game over the Valley for more than four hours, passed over, the thunder rolling away, stumbling like a drunken giant across the hills to the south-west. Soon the dampness rose in misty whiteness from the ground, drifting slowly upwards and back into the humid atmosphere.

Swilila stretched towards her baby and vigorously licked him all over; as she did so the sun burst through a break in the scurrying clouds, dappling golden flashes over his damp coat. He staggered upright and tottered on tiny hooves, trying to shake the brightness from his eyes, the sudden movements toppling him to the ground once more. Then he stood again, sharply, breaking the umbilical cord with an almost audible snap.

Still lying, Swilila cleaned up her birth-site and herself, removing the tell-tale scents, watching her son rise and fall several times until, only a short while after birth, his legs sustained his weight. He began probing for his mother's udder, overshooting time and time again before reaching the life-giving target, and his little tail flittered rapidly from side to side as the warm milk began to fill his belly.

The impala herd had grouped closer together, and paused in its feeding while the afternoon storm had blustered around them. Now individuals began to move about again within the area of their narrow home territory, bounded on one side by the sloping shore of the river, marked on others by Mwami's dominant scent stamped out from the glands under the tufts of black hair which grew low on his hind legs.

Mwami was a handsome old ram, standing tall for an impala. His coat was deeper red than most, and the white

throat and belly unusually whiter. The characteristic warning pattern of black and white on his buttocks was sharply defined, and flashed conspicuously whenever he led the herd from danger. His beautiful, lyre horns were worn smooth in places where he had rubbed against trees, and were chipped from the scars of innumerable battles. One had been broken at the tip several years ago when he had helped to release a young otter, trapped by the tail beneath a fallen tree. He moved with a slow dignity which commanded respect from all others of his species, even those outside his own select clan; and now he detached himself from them, walking to the edge of the mopane thicket where he knew Swilila to be.

They talked, these two impalas, in the language of their kind: soft sounds which matched the meaning of their thoughts, though their mouths did not move to form the words.

"A fine mulombe," said the leader, and tossed his head in a gesture of approval. "Best I've seen for a long time. You did well, Swilila, you did indeed."

He could have said, truthfully, "we did well", but it was not in his nature to take credit for what, after all, was only his duty for the continuation of his highly-bred herd. After his comment, unusually generous even for an occasion like this, he turned to go. But Swilila called him back, politely.

"O Mwami," she spoke shyly, "I have a feeling in my heart that this one" — she dropped her gaze to her son who was quite oblivious of Mwami's regal presence — "this one is special, like yourself, and I have named him Kali-Anuka."

"Brave and wise?" He dwelt on the words, and slowly raised his head to grasp a succulent mouthful of fresh, green mopane leaves from a near-by branch. He repeated the words again and again as he munched. "Yes," he said at last, "as that is the feeling you have about this new mulombe, it must have come to you from Fura-Uswa, the godkin to the animals of the Great Valley. Kali-Anuka... Kali-Anuka ..." he mused. "Eyaa! ... I have known of  few impalas able to live up to such a name, but from what I hear we may need one or two such paragons before long. Yes,

Swilila, you may name him Kali-Anuka, and let us hope he will live up to his name. Ko caala, Swilila, farewell!"

She watched him as he walked away, proud horned head slightly bowed in, it seemed to her, troubled thought. And she was uneasy.

"Ka sike, Mwami!" she called softly.

She turned to her lamb, but the uncomfortable feeling did not go away. She licked and nuzzled him as he pulled hungrily at her udder, and when he let go, satisfied at last, she walked the few paces to the mopane tree, reaching up with her long, graceful neck to set about stripping the butterfly-wing leaves from the branches above her head. They still dripped with cool moisture from the departed storm.

She thought about her closest friend, the talkative Silulimi who, she was sure, would have a lot to say about her new lamb. She would not mind, for Silulimi had given birth to a female earlier in the lambing season, and the youngster was now over six weeks old; there would be much to discuss. As she was the first-born, Silulimi had called her Kusomona.

The afternoon shadows, grey from the mist-veiled sun, were lengthening as Silulimi and her daughter moved through the herd, busy with everyday activities, towards Swilila's birth-site. Her friend knew the place exactly, and remembered when the more experienced mother had told her how important it was, when birth pains started, to move discreetly out of sight of the herd to an area well-shielded by bushes and long grass. This was a survival technique which Swilila had learnt only after the arrival of her second lamb, born in open ground.

"Wa buka? How are you, Swilila?" her friend asked as she approached, glancing admiringly at Kali-Anuka, who was again suckling. The two does nuzzled each other in greeting.

"I am well," Swilila replied. With a note of pride in her voice, she added: "and Mwami has said I may call my son Kali-Anuka."

"Ah-ha!" Silulimi exclaimed, knowingly. "I take it that Mwami is the little lamb's father, or he wouldn't have agreed so readily?"

Swilila nodded, and smiled with her eyes. "Yes," she said, "for the first time."

"Good for the old ram! Of course," Silulimi went on, "I've known for a long time he's been trying for a son to take over when he's deposed, or dies, or something. No wonder he didn't object to such a high-flying name. Kali-Anuka, eh? — it must have given him quite a kick!"

"Oh, Silulimi! — you shouldn't be so disrespectful." Then, with a worried stamp of a front hoof, she said: "I'm so troubled with something, something Mwami spoke of — or at least, hinted at."

Her friend's ears came forward, flapping, her interest aroused, and Swilila told her what he had said.

"My dear, you know what an old worrier he is!" commented Silulimi. "He's always fretting about all the terrible things that could happen to us and, the good Fura-Uswa knows, we have enough without thinking up new ones."

While the does had been talking, Kusomona, who was too young for conversation, investigated Kali-Anuka, thrusting her muzzle up against his white throat as he suckled, licking and nuzzling at his fresh, young coat.

"I must go back," Silulimi said at last, "or Mwami will come looking for me. Come, Kusomona," giving her daughter a gentle prod with her nose, "there'll be plenty of time to get to know Kali-Anuka later on."

Swilila walked a few paces with her; then, alone with her lamb, grazed on a clump of couch-grass. Through the patchy undergrowth she could see, as she pulled at the scaly rhizomes, some of the herd moving off slowly towards the clearing where they usually rested at night. They were safer in the open; in dense bush it was more difficult to see, smell and hear the approach of an enemy.

Far away up in the hills came the rasping grunts of a pair of leopards. Swilila raised her head, and her ears came forward, instantly alert. But she decided there was no immediate danger and lay down, close under an acacia bush, and ruminated herself into sleep. Kali-Anuka, his little golden body now supported firmly on his legs, ran in circles round his

mother until he dropped exhausted beside her, and fell asleep
with his head resting on her neck.

The storm on that December day of Kali-Anuka's birth
was the forerunner of many summer storms to come. For
nearly half a year they would lour angrily from the north,
bursting savagely over the valley, sometimes every day,
shaking the ground as the driving winds slammed the rain
across the smooth surface of the wide river. Everything would
seem to drown, and then, quickly, like the sudden flinging
open of a giant furnace door, the sun would blaze down, and
steam would rise in pale mists from the sodden ground until
all was dry again. The dense forests of acacia and mopane, the
impenetrable jesse bush and the towering mahogany trees
on the river banks, rested under the hot sun, awaiting the next
deluge. The roots of tall grasses and lush green turf, here and
there cropped to the smoothness of an English lawn, thirstily
drank the moisture and waited for more.

For all free-running animals life is perilous, and yet in its
way, idyllic. Antelopes do not have to fight for their food, and
impalas are no exception; their purpose in life is to survive, to
stay alive by finding a mate and leaving progeny to fill the
gaps left by those who die, from whatever cause. On the
whole, Mwami and his herd managed very well.

He was an old ram, approaching eleven years, and for the
past seven he had borne the mantle of supreme authority over
his small, select community. At this time he headed seven
rams, twenty-four does and, with the recent addition of Kali-
Anuka, four lambs. Five of the does were pregnant and would
be dropping their young within a few days of each other; —
then the little herd would be increased, at least temporarily,
to forty-one head. Until the next lambing season, this figure
could only diminish to a number governed by the frequency of
attack by predators, sickness, drowning by flood, and killing
by man, the creature they most feared, who carried the long
sticks which exploded at the same time that death came.

There was something rather special about Mwami's
herd, as though there were some unknown destiny for them to

fulfil. At a distant point in their evolution, the ancestors of Mwami must have split off from the rest, and established themselves as an independent breeding population. Rarely was an outsider allowed entry; he would have to be a bachelor ram, personally selected by the leader himself who was very particular, for there must be no threat to his leadership, or risk of lowering the high quality of breeding.

Neighbouring herds respected the Pambuka, so-called because of their higher intelligence and aloofness. They kept as much as possible to themselves, spending their lives feeding and ruminating, drinking, grooming and sleeping a little. Appropriate to sex and season, they mated, gave birth and suckled their young. In the rutting season, the rams

fought one another over the does, parrying and thrusting with their horns like swordsmen; but these duels seldom resulted in serious injury, and very rarely in death. For the most part they exercised the normal behaviour of other impalas, but the Pambuka's uniqueness was in its high degree of communication and its permanence, combining to develop an unusually close relationship between individuals.

To the animals who suffered from man's frightening and often tragic indignities, it was merciful that they did not happen with great frequency in this part of the Great Valley. Many months could go by with little activity by the Zimikile, as they were known by the impalas because of their strange, upright posture. It came mostly from those with the thin mouths; the darker, full-lipped ones killed, but usually only for food, or skins for clothing; and during the rains, when they kept to their villages close to the river and fished, there was hardly sight or scent of them.

For the past two or three years, however, there had been more movement and activity in the valley by both species than ever before. Although none of it had, as yet, affected the Pambuka who confined themselves to the territory near the river, Mwami had knowledge of much killing of animals of all kinds, and destruction of bush and woodland in places high in the hills. Great birds, bigger and noisier than any which had frequented the valley before, had been seen and heard flying low over the land, their wings rigid and unbeating. Sometimes a mist issued from their bowels, killing all insects touched by it, in the air or on the ground. They died in their hundreds of thousands, in their millions. Animals eating the insects became ill, and often died. There were stories of many gatherings of the dark-faced Zimikile of the Batonka tribes who lived in the valley, and of angry talk between them and those others with the paler faces.

What concerned Mwami most of all were the tales of whole herds of impala wiped out by explosions from those deadly Zimikile sticks; not only impalas, but nearly all the larger species of animals. He wondered, fearfully, when the trail of slaughter and destruction would reach close to the river, though he could not guess at the purpose of it.

One day, when the sun was falling quickly through the clouds, down towards its setting, the impalas went to their favourite place, a narrow sandy beach flanked by woodland, handy for cover in case of danger. They loved it here; there were good salt-licks, and up against the small, flat rocks on the sand grew tufts of sweet grass which they relished more than any other. Although they would strip every delicate blade of it, more would shoot up overnight to provide another feast on the next day. It was so pleasant here, late in the afternoons or in the mornings, when insects were less troublesome in the river-cooled air. During the dry season they drank at the beach until the rains came again, when all the moisture they needed was in the food they ate.

A little way upstream, a family of hippopotamus wallowed in the deep, reedy water; a mother and her calf grazed on a thick clump of grass which grew on the bank where the strip of sand ended. From the heap of heaving hippos in the water, two old bulls detached themselves to fight together, lazily and with little effect.

Then, from downstream and distantly, Mwami's keen ears picked up the steady, high-pitched throb of one of the carrier-creatures used by the Zimikile when they travelled on water. He was familiar with these creatures, but more so with the ones which made no sound, ridden by the black Zimikile when out on the river, fishing.

As the sound grew louder the hippos silently submerged, the cow pushed her calf unceremoniously into the water, and followed just as the small carrier appeared round the bend in the river. The impalas stood alert and ready for Mwami's warning snort which would signal danger, and send them instantly to cover. The carrier turned from midstream, drifting towards the shore as the throbbing sound diminished to an irregular clatter. There were four Zimikile sitting on it, two of them pale and thin-lipped. One stood up, steadying himself as he raised his gun. All at once Mwami snorted, the gun exploded, and an unweaned lamb dropped to the sand.

The impalas fled in frantic leaps back into the trees, and later the little dead lamb was carried to the boat, and dumped carelessly in the forward well.

2

IT was believed beyond doubt by every member of Mwami's herd, and by all the animals and birds of the Great Valley, that the godkin who watched over them was the spirit of Fura-Uswa, the grass-eater, a white rhinoceros who had lived and died in the valley many years before.

He had been the last of a species which had thrived, though never in very great numbers. His near relative, the black, or hook-lipped rhino, had been more successful because he was wilder and more aggressive. But the square-lipped white rhino was a gentle, trusting creature despite his greater bulk, and was therefore easier game for human hunters. First the black men; then, from their earliest days of venturing into the Zambezi valley with their guns and sophisticated methods, the white men.

So, by early in this century, there were no more white rhinos in the valley, except for one. And he, the last to bear the name Fura-Uswa, soon fell to a white man's bullet. But his restless spirit survived, to keep vigil over all other animals and birds, eternally dedicated to use his powers in preserving every existing species, and in bitter hostility against all men who, collectively, caused the extermination of his own kind.

When a man, black or white, sets his trap to catch an animal in its cruel grip, and later comes to see what rich prize he has won, only to find the trap closed over nothing but air, this is, perhaps, the work of Fura-Uswa. Or when a boastful hunter, who considers himself a crack shot, aims to bring down his victim with a bullet to that fatal spot between the eyes, and misses, it is possible that Fura-Uswa has interfered with its trajectory. But few men know of this and, if they do, most would not believe it. It was believed by the Pambuka, and all other animals and birds of the Great Valley.

The Pambuka impalas also believed (though Mwami himself was sceptical) that the spirit of Fura-Uswa dwelt within Tantalika the otter, on occasion; that he was the

medium appointed by the godkin to watch over all impalas in the valley, but particularly those of the Pambuka herd, for they were special and few in number, to be protected more than any others.

They believed he was chosen because it was his nature never to remain in one place for long, spending his life roaming the vast territory, across land and through water, familiarising himself with all that took place, often able to warn his defenceless friends of threatened danger that otherwise might have befallen them. And it must be said that Tantalika took great delight in deliberately fostering and encouraging this belief of his special powers, and his relationship with the godkin, for there were always some, like Mwami, who remained unconvinced.

He led a lonely life, for there were not many otters in the valley, and his close alliance with the impalas was something he cherished and wanted to hold for the rest of his days. His friendship with the Pambuka had come about when he had been a cub, not long independent of his parents, and the only survivor of a litter of three. He had been clumsily chasing a young spring hare, losing it as it fled down the entrance to its burrow, when the heavy branch of a dead rain-tree had fallen from the ravages of termites, pinning his tail to the flat rock upon which he sat. Mwami found him, and with another ram they lifted the branch with their fragile horns, risking breakage, just enough for the little otter to slip his tail from the trap between rough bark and hard rock. As Mwami lowered the branch, too quickly, the tip of one of his horns snapped off. After that, his head ached for many days.

Tantalika would have starved to death, or been easy meat for some predator, had it not been for these two, and he had not only befriended the old ram and all his herd (the other rescuer had long since died), but ever since then felt he owed a debt of gratitude which he tried to repay in many ways. But in his heart, and despite his subsequent visitation and appointment as go-between by Fura-Uswa, he knew he never could.

Mwami taught him to speak impala language, and they spent many happy hours together before Tantalika was able to converse in simple phrases. He found it difficult to adapt his voice to the soft tones an impala understands, for otter language is made up of many sounds — whistles and chirrups, hissing, whining, squeaks and growls — all running over each other in a continuous kind of double-talk. But at last he overcame his disadvantage, and when Mwami decided he was ready, he called other impalas to join in conversation so that all could, with practice, communicate with the otter, and he with them.

Many happy moments passed by thus, with the impalas formed in a rough circle, lying or standing, the diminutive Tantalika at the centre, as though he were teacher and not pupil, telling one another stories handed down through

generations, or of new experiences which would be told, and retold, again and again. They talked of the curious ways of other animals; of the hippopotamus who wags his tail when defecating, scattering his dung over a wide area; of how he sinks to the bottom of the river, and trots along the bed with ease. Enviously, they spoke of elephants' ears, those leaf-like flaps which cool the air and drive away the swarms of insects that disturb their peace; their tree-branch trunks which swing high in the air to catch the messages of the wind. They thought it strange that warthogs, who often shared their grazing, should be so ugly, and yet such pleasant companions. Was it awareness of their ugliness that made them kneel to eat, as though in humble thanks to their creator for sparing them good things with which to fill their bellies?

Sometimes, when the shadows of day melted into twilight, darkening under the trees, they talked of the beauty of the world they lived in: of white clouds sailing over the valley, of moonglow bright on the river, and the cool taste of water after rain; of shining stars falling, burning paths across the night sky; of the marbled glory of a summer sunset; of hearing bird-songs tossed from tree to tree, and the wing-beats of waterfowl migrating from one edge of the world to the other; or the sweet scent of mopane leaves; the freshness of a winter dawn; the perfection of a new-born lamb.

Then, perhaps, as night fell, they would talk of some of the unbeautiful things: of wild rain falling, and thunderclaps that shake the world; of fire burning through grass, and flame-strangled trees; of flood, and famine when only dry, bare stalks are left for sustenance; the pain of disease, or injury; the bloodless end from a plague of parasites; the mad glow in the eyes of a lioness before the kill; the scent of man, the fear of death, and death itself . . . the long, everlasting silence.

Tantalika learned fast, but it was a long time before the others could understand him.

The name 'Tantalika' means, approximately, 'he who moves quickly, like a spider'. He certainly moved quickly, quicker in water than on land, but in appearance he was less like a spider than anything else imaginable. He had a long, sturdy body, his pointed tail half its length, and his muzzle was whiskered and mous-
tached. On each side of his
head were ridiculously
small, though very sensi-
tive ears. He really looked
no different from otters
anywhere else in the world,
except that his feet had no
claws, and while others'
were webbed, his were not.

He was always full of
fun, although so much of
his life was spent alone. He loved playing tricks on his friends, even those who should be treated with respect and a certain amount of reverence, like Mwami.

The old ram was getting a bit stiff in his joints these days, and liked to loosen up sometimes, jogging in circles, or chasing the young females. One day, after exercising, puffed and hot, he went to drink at a pool left by the swollen river late in the season. Suddenly he was startled, but not surprised, when Tantalika dropped into the water, close to his mouth. Mwami looked up, shaking droplets from his eyes.

"I'm pleased to see you, Tantalika, as always," he said, a little stiffly, "but I would be happier if you'd make your entrance in a more conventional manner."

The otter trod water, and wiggled his whiskers.

"I just dropped in to ask if there have been any Zimikile seen in your territory, Mwami," he said, ignoring the impala's greeting. "They seem to be getting everywhere else."

Mwami told him about the water-borne men, and the killing of the lamb; but there was nothing more to add.

"You will see much of them soon, when the season of Gandapati and the falling of leaves begins. Already, up and down the river, they are busy with things which are difficult to understand, and on the banks — far away from them sometimes — they make their camps and journey to and from them every day."

"And the killing of animals and birds and insects, away from the river? Does that still go on?" Mwami asked anxiously.

"Yes, Mwami — and worse than before."

By now Tantalika had edged himself out of the pool, and stood beside Mwami, balanced three-pointed on broad tail and hind feet. He scratched his nose, and sneezed twice.

"Fura-Uswa is very angry," he said, "and believes the Zimikile may wish to destroy the valley and everything in it. He wants me to travel to the place where the river falls from the sky into a deep chasm, then back along the Great Valley until the river shrinks, and passes through the gorge of Kariba. There I must report to him about all I have seen, and then he will talk things over with Nyaminyami, the river god who is known only to the black Zimikile."

"Nyaminyami?" queried Mwami. "I have not heard of this one."

"I know little of him," Tantalika said, lowering his voice. "Fura-Uswa has told me only that he is the spirit of a monster, a great snake who lived in the river long, long before Fura-Uswa was born. His whiskers tickle the clouds to make the rain come, and his coils push the water away to make the floods."

"M'm — sounds a bit far-fetched, I must say," said Mwami.

Tantalika, a little piqued by this remark, was in too much of a hurry for argument. Omitting any farewell words, he ran off into the bush and was quickly out of sight.

Impalas do not frown when they are worried, but stamp a front hoof once, or many times, depending on the depth of their anxiety. Now, despite his scepticism, Mwami stamped his hoof so many times that it hammered a hole in the hard ground. Although, as always, he had listened to all the otter had said with a lick of salt, he was not so foolish as to dismiss it as complete fantasy. There was, without doubt, cause for disquiet. He looked across at his herd, and wondered what, if anything, he should tell them.

They stood or lay in groups at the edge of the clearing, some foraging for food, others grooming, and the younger ones at play. Swilila and her friend Silulimi lay together gossiping, eyes ever watchful on their offspring as they chased one another in small, bucking circles, a short distance away. With sidelong glances at the youngsters, Mwami walked over to the two does; they moved to rise as he approached.

"Don't get up," he said.

Before he could say anything else, he was interrupted by a sudden rustling nearby, and the voice of Tantalika.

"I forgot to tell you when I'll return," he said, standing between the resting does and their leader.

Mwami raised his head. "When will that be?"

"When many moons have passed, and the clouds are again heavy with rain," said the otter, and dashed off, without another word, to join Kali-Anuka and Kusomona in their game.

"Not until then?" called Mwami.

Diving in and out between the leaping legs of the youngsters in a game he had invented himself, Tantalika shouted back: "Not until then!" and streaked off towards the river, running with arched back, zigzagging through the forest of legs, scattering the impalas, mock-startled, in all directions.

"That's a long time to wait," Mwami said, almost to himself. As he walked away, having forgotten what he had decided to tell the does, Silulimi leaned towards her friend.

"What *is* going on?" she asked quietly. "I've been trying to find out, but no one seems to know anything. I'm sure Mwami was about to tell us when that silly otter butted in. It's most terribly disappointing."

"But what are you trying to find out, Silulimi dear?"

"That's the trouble — I don't know. There's *something* going on, of that I'm sure. You remember the day Kali-Anuka was born" — she glanced over at the sturdy young juvenile, now almost six months old and still growing — "and you told me that Mwami had said something to trouble you? A premonition, you said, of disaster."

"Well," Swilila smiled, "we had that with the last floods, didn't we?"

"Oh no — *that* was nothing! We're all still here, aren't we? Or most of us. And floods come nearly every year." She thought for a moment, then said: "Do you know what *I* think? I believe it's something to do with Zimikile. Mwami said, you told me, there will be need for 'brave and wise' impalas —

what could he *possibly* mean by that? We all know we're not brave, or wise, or ever likely to be. We're beautiful, yes, if we accept the opinion of warthogs, though anything is beautiful to them, poor things. I grant you we're not quite stupid, but we're about the most defenceless creatures in the valley. Look at our rams — lovely, curving horns, marvellously defiant in the face of danger, and sharp enough to rip through to the heart of a lion."

Swilila shivered at the thought.

"Yes, my dear — but you shiver and shake because you know our rams would never try and attack anything, let alone a lion. And if they did, those wonderful horns would snap off like dry twigs!"

"But Mwami doesn't always run away," Swilila said defensively.

"I grant you that. But it's his duty as a leader — or dominant male as he likes to call himself — to act as decoy. He's getting too old and unappetising for doing *that* with any success, these days."

"Mwami is brave," said Swilila, flatly. "Mwami is also wise, and so Kali-Anuka will be, I promise you."

"Oh Swilila, my dearest friend, how I hope you'll be proved right! But however exceptional an impala ram Kali-Anuka turns out to be, I want to know *now* what it is Mwami is keeping from us. His silence and the rumours are only leading to a greater fear among us all. You know the old impala saying: 'you must see how deep the river is before crossing it'. Well, if we *knew*, we could at least be sure whether we'll be able to cross it or not."

3

WHEN Tantalika set forth on his journey, his intention was, of course, to keep his appointment with Fura-Uswa. But this was not to be until the next rains, and he had many months before then to roam the valley, gathering information on the activities of men, so that he could report them to the godkin, as he had been instructed.

He also made up his mind to take this opportunity to search for a mate.

Since the separation from his mother over five years ago, he had not encountered another member of his species in the area of his birth. On occasions when he had ventured further afield, he had met with a few, but never an unattached female. Except once, when a she-otter long past her youth, bit his nose so violently that he decided to have nothing more to do with her. Now, he resolved, it was time to redouble his efforts to find a mate, and after his talk with Mwami, he travelled south-west, upstream, and on to the broad plains which rolled away from each side of the river, the flatness broken here and there with gently undulating hills.

He did not find what he was looking for, but he saw the great Zimikile birds casting their deadly mist over the countryside. He heard the explosions from the rifles, and when all was quiet again, he went down into the shallow valleys, feeling the hush of death over everything, seeing the animal carrion rotting in the sun, food for the scavengers, and more than they could cope with.

Failing to discover an object for his frustrated affections, and distressed with the sights and sounds he had encountered, he moved downstream, north-east towards the place where the hills suddenly pressed in on the river to form a narrow gorge; and he came upon other things which, if anything, he found more disturbing.

After resting a few days in his holt under the bank across the river from the Pambuka herd's regular drinking place, he set off downstream once more. Not so much, now, to seek a mate, but to look for other signs of destruction by the Zimikile.

He kept to the water at first, sometimes swimming slowly on the surface, paddling without effort, dog-fashion; sometimes moving swiftly, throwing his whole body into strenuous action, shooting himself forward in a curving motion, with his tail switching strongly, acting as propeller and rudder at the same time.

After a long spell underwater at a very wide section of the river, he surfaced to fill his lungs with new air, and his acute hearing picked up a roaring sound from high ground inland from the south bank. To him it suggested a large number of carrier-creatures, and he could see, billowing up towards the cloudless sky, a thick haze of dust. His sensitive nose was assailed by an abnoxious smell, new in his experience. Venting air, he dived again, deeply, turned for the shore and, unerring in his submarine navigation, surfaced in the still, shallow water of a sheltered inlet overhung with tall, riverine vegetation. He paddled ashore, sliding through loopholes in the dense tangle of tree roots, and wriggled away through the bush.

The roaring noise grew louder as he approached higher ground, and seemed to roll towards him, pushing the very air aside, flattening his small round ears against the stiff fur of his head. Several times he stopped, nose pointed up, sniffing the scent of men mingling with the other smell. He reached the top of the rise, and in a flurry of dust, stones, bushes and dry branches, he saw before him a massive chain, each link of it larger than himself, scouring across the ground. At first he was completely bewildered, frozen into immobility by fear; then he saw, attached to each end of the long chain, a huge steel ball as big as an elephant. Both rolled in the same direction as the chain, bouncing heavily so that he could feel the vibrations  under his paws. He watched, incredulous, as a spinney of white syringas, no more than two tree lengths away, toppled down together in a shower of leaves and snapping branches, their thick roots dragged out mercilessly from the subsoil.

Even with his high intelligence, Tantalika could not understand the purpose of what was happening before his eyes; but when he peered beyond the fallen trees, and saw a black-faced Zimikile astride a giant carrier bigger and uglier than any he had yet seen, he realised at once that this evil noise and the striking down of the trees was new and certain evidence of the incomprehensible Zimikile plan to destroy the Great Valley — and everything in it.

He stood rigid, the hair on his back raised, his long tail held straight. Only his nostrils moved as they worked at the scents drifting across from the devastation before him. To his left, not far away, the ground rose again steeply, and partly to escape the assault on his ears and whole body he ran as fast as his short legs would allow up the slope, dodging in and out of the thick scrub, until he reached an open promontory. From there, he stared down on to an area of destruction, where hundreds of trees lay broken, limply dying, with others falling to the dragging, rasping chains. Clouds of blue-grey smoke rose high into the breathless air from several points, where stacks of green timber burned away to ashes.

Although no tears fell from his eyes, Tantalika wept, with little whimpering cries which came from his aching heart. Here, in the land where he had dwelt all his life, the comfortable landscape was changing, for no reason he could think of, except to satisfy the inexplicable whim of the Zimikile. And for the first time in his life he felt a sense of loss. With an overwhelming desire to escape the dust and smoke, the noise and unpleasant smells, he turned and ran helter-skelter down to the river.

He took a different trail back to the shore, knowing that the river curved in a wide sweep south before flowing north-east again; he would thus save time by taking the short cut overland, and he longed to enjoy moving through familiar woodland before, perhaps, it was all lost forever.

Like all otters, Tantalika was happiest in his natural element, water. On land he could, however, move over long distances, although his short legs had their limitations. He travelled rapidly, walking or running, rolling or sliding now and then, according to the suitability of the terrain.

Pausing only to snatch a fat insect or two, warding off the pangs of hunger, he made good progress and hoped to reach the river before sunset. Then he could enjoy a fish dinner before settling down for the night in some river-side hole, or a crevice in the rocks.

He rustled noisily through deep drifts of dead, dry leaves, revelling in the sound; over wide, boulder-strewn stretches of rough ground, he leapt from rock to rock with the nimbleness of a klipspringer.

He never felt alone when he travelled on land. The valley was always full of life, and as he cut across open vlei, or dodged through dense forest, he came across many species.

Elephant and rhinoceros, big as they were, did not harrass him, the former gentle by nature, the latter too cumbersome and clumsy for chasing otters. He was wary of snakes and the big cats, and once, with the wind behind him, he failed to hear or scent lion. Cleaving through tall, yellow grass, he suddenly found himself in the middle of a pride of sleeping lions. But they were satiated from the meat of a buffalo carcass nearby, and slept on.

Late in the afternoon he came across a forest trail made by human feet, and knew that if he followed it he would reach a place where black Zimikile lived. He did not fear them, for their homes, like those of all other creatures in the Great Valley, had always been part of it. So he kept to the trail, hoping there might be food to steal at the end of it.

Once before he had entered a village of the Batonka, seeking a meal of chicken, for a change. His foray had been unsuccessful, for he had been chased away by thin dogs, big, almost naked women, and laughing children. In the confusion, goats had scattered, bleating, in all directions. With the fun of it he had forgotten his hunger and later satisfied himself with a snack of two toads he had found hibernating in the hollow trunk of a tree. He remembered the incident well, for he had been fascinated, in the limited time he had for exploration before discovery, with the bustling activity of the place. Children ran about playing and shouting, while the women, beaded and bangled, with sticks or porcupine quills stuck through their noses, pounded corn, laughing, talking and singing all the time. Their hair was smeared with red-ochre paste, and Tantalika could smell the strong animal smell of the fat spread on their skin. At the nearby shore the men stood waist-deep in the water, fishing with hook and line; others cleaned the few fish they had caught, then hung them to dry on long bamboo poles. He remembered thinking that if only all Zimikile were like these, there would be little to fear from them.

He thought of this again as he trotted along the path, passing a patch of corn; he was sharp enough to notice that the plants were wilting in the dusty, unwatered soil. He went

on, slower now, nostrils working, trying to detect man-scent.
Rounding a corner, he came suddenly on the village. But
there was no sign of life; no dogs barked at him menacingly, no
children played their primitive games, no men or women
busied themselves at their daily chores. It was a small village,

even for Batonka. Just a cluster of huts on a patch of bare
earth stamped hard by many feet. The huts were round and
thatched, built of poles or wickerwork and mud; some, used
for storing corn, stood precariously on stilts. A few discarded
drinking gourds lay about. But only the lapping of the river,
and the faint rustling of the wind in nearby trees broke the
silence.

Tantalika's keen eyes caught movement beneath one of
the stilted huts, but it was only a family of cane rats scrabbling
for grain which had fallen through the floor to the ground. A
fish-eagle swooped low, gliding silently overhead, but flew on,
soaring upwards over the river, head thrown right back calling
his "kow-kowkow-kow-kow". Standing at his full height the

otter felt a new unease; now it was with the disappearance of
some of the valley people from their homes.

Glad to put some distance between himself and the
abandoned village, he ran down to the shore, staying in the
shallows until he caught a fish, and with it securely clamped
between his teeth, he draped himself over a smooth rock and
began eating.

Over on the opposite shore, an elephant trumpeted.
Baboons and monkeys barked and chattered; hippos snorted,
and through the evening bird-song a hornbill hooted un-
melodiously, the water dikkops whistled, and upriver a pair of
fish-eagles yelped as they soared across from bank to bank.

Tantalika listened to all these and other comforting,
familiar sounds, and watched as the river ran in great streams
of flame under the setting sun. Night came quickly, the
distant hills turned purple, and the valleys filled with heavy
shadows. How long, he wondered, before all this might be
gone, just as those valley people, the animals and trees he had
seen, had already gone?

In the weeks that followed, as he travelled further away
to the north-east, sometimes overland but more frequently
along the course of the river, Tantalika came upon more
deserted villages and heard again the awful clamour of tree-
killing, but it was distant for he could not bring himself close
enough to witness it again.

Twice he came across roads — the wide, hardened trails
made by the Zimikile — and on both occasions there were
carriers moving along them, heavily laden with long, branch-
less tree-trunks, or crammed with black people, sitting or
lying uncomfortably among their goats and dogs and meagre
possessions.

As the great heat of Kavumbi, the month of October,
pressed down on the valley, he tired of venturing far from the
river, and laid up where the current flowed fast and cool,
finding a long-deserted otter holt, littered with the discarded
remains of shell foods. It was close to a sheltered beach, rich

with crabs and mussels, on the edge of a shady inlet — a promising fishing ground. He enjoyed himself there, and it was not until the level of the river rose with the heavy rains that he moved on, reluctantly, to keep his appointment with Fura-Uswa.

Soon he could no longer keep to the river. It flowed too fiercely, even for an otter, where it began to narrow as it entered the long gorge. He scrambled over submerged rocks which long ago had tumbled down from the steep banks; but this was hard going, and his paws were sore and bleeding. So up the hillside, through the dense woodland he went, hurrying although there was no need. But he was sensing the closeness of some awful catastrophe and hearing, faintly, a confusion of sounds, many of which he had never heard before. Over all, the familiar roar of carrier-creatures funnelled along the narrow confines of the gorge.

He reached the top of another long, low hill, but could see nothing for trees. For a while he scouted about, at last breaking through into a clearing just below the summit on the far side. All the time the cacophony stayed with him, louder and louder, until it rang in his ears. Once in the clearing, he had an almost uninterrupted view of the constricted river as it twisted through the gorge, but to see a little further, he stood up to his full height.

He knew at once what was he saw, and what, eventually, it would bring about. His immediate assessment was not an intelligent guess; it came from stored-up knowledge of generations of otters who knew of another animal — a rodent — which lived in places far, far distant from the Great Valley. Like himself, they spent most of their lives in water. They felled trees in early summer, gnawing at them, using the logs for building dams across rivers and streams, filling the gaps with leaves and mud, so that the barrier held back the water to form a small lake, trapping fish for winter feeding, and ensuring a playground for their young, born in the spring.

But this monstrous structure across the gorge was no beaver dam; and, certainly, it was not built of logs. Great solid towers straddled one side of the river bed, almost as high as the flanking hills, and a long wall, already half-damming the river's flow, curved in a wide arc around the towers. The river surged through the gap between the wall and towers, and the other bank, spreading out again beyond to continue its interrupted course, passing beneath two frail bridges which spanned its width.

Cut into the hills on both banks was a maze of trails, with noisy carrier-creatures moving back and forth, kicking up the thick red mud with their whirling, circular feet. Although Tantalika stood a long way from all this, the noises reached him clearly — the carriers, the high or low-pitched whining of unknown man-machines, the clattering of others, banging and thumping; and sometimes even the shouting voices of the many men who, busy as dung-beetles at a midden, swarmed everywhere.

Up on his vantage point Tantalika heard the rain coming, first on a gentle breeze rustling the trees around him, then carried on fierce gusts, a hissing, lashing deluge, penetrating his coarse outer fur, stinging the skin beneath. Usually he loved the rain, especially when he was on land; but now he longed for a dry place to rest, where he could nurse his damaged paws.

He climbed down the hillside, and soon found a narrow burrow under a steep bank which ensured that for however long the rain lasted, he could rest, snug and warm in the dry. But he was not at all happy with his situation. The discomfort he felt in such close proximity to so many Zimikile, not unmixed with fear, was hard to bear. He wished he could go to Fura-Uswa in the morning, but the godkin had not yet informed him when to come or, for that matter, exactly where to go.

The rain fell heavily and continuously for three days and nights, and Tantalika did not emerge from his burrow except to snatch a few mouthfuls of damp insects, and an unpalatable lizard.

On the fourth day, when the rain had slackened to a steady drizzle, he watched for hours as the river below swelled into a raging torrent, sweeping down from the Great Valley, building up its strength against the high curved wall and the huge, solid towers of the dam. He watched the men increase their activities, working desperately in little groups to strengthen the ends of the two bridges further downstream, for the river was hurling its lashing waves at them, but not high enough yet to sweep them away. The grey rain deadened the sounds of men and machines; Tantalika could hear only the rushing, roaring water, and it seemed to him that nothing could withstand its terrible force.

Incredulously he stared, hardly daring to breathe, as a long wave heaved over the curved wall, poured itself into the maelstrom below, then threw itself against the first bridge. It disintegrated as though constructed of twigs, and was swept away in small pieces downriver. The second bridge, a stronger affair, vanished beneath the wave but reappeared, showering streams of water from its edges. But it remained intact.

Suddenly, as though some unseen hand had signalled,

the onslaught seemed to be over. A turbulent arc of foam marked the position of the dam wall underwater, and though the torrent continued to pour through the gorge, where the dam had been, the level began to fall.

For a long time Tantalika stood under the wet, misty sky, marvelling at what he had seen, and wondered if, perhaps, the assault on the dam had been the work of Fura-Uswa . . . or Nyaminyami. He was soon to know.

On the day when Tantalika first set eyes on the dam at Kariba, and heard the rain coming from the north-east, the sun was blazing down from a clear sky many miles away, upriver. Everything seemed normal that morning, and when Mwami and his impalas went down to the beach where the sweet grass grew, they hardly noticed a slight rise in the level of the river since the previous day. They did not go down at all on the next day, for heavy rain had fallen during the night and well into the morning; they were content to feed on the grass where they stood. But when they trailed again to the beach on the following morning, it had disappeared, the sheltering trees stood an impala's height in water and, to Mwami's amazement, the usual steady flow of the river was stilled. He looked closer, and it seemed that the current had reversed, moving almost imperceptibly upstream instead of down.

This cannot be, he thought, or has the world somehow tilted the other way? He lifted his head to the sky and he could see, dimly, the pattern of black and grey clouds far away to the north-east, heavy with rain. He shifted his gaze to the opposite bank, and there, too, some of the trees were partly submerged.

Only twice before in his long life could he remember seeing such rapid flooding; but both times the river had increased the speed of its flow, not diminished it — and certainly not turned it about.

He began to wonder when Tantalika would return. Perhaps it was something to do with Fura-Uswa, or with the Zimikile, and although he was reluctant to accept the possibility, the otter might have some explanation to offer for such a strange phenomenon. He had said he would return 'when the clouds are again heavy with rain'. They were now, most days, but it would not be long before the rainfall would dwindle to an occasional showery storm, and the long dry months of winter would begin again.

A handsome ram of more than two years, who had earned the name of Yandika for his friendliness, came up quietly behind Mwami.

"What do you make of it, Yandika?" asked Mwami.

"A lot of rain downriver," the young ram said, and moved to Mwami's side. "But I don't think we'll get it today."

Mwami stamped a hoof irritably.

"No, no, Yandika — I mean the river. Look — look how wide and full it is. I have seldom seen it come up so fast, and can't you notice something strange?"

Yandika lifted a back hoof to scratch his chin.

"Well," he said, "we're in for a bit of a flood, I suppose. But it shouldn't last long."

"But can't you see? Can't you see it's flowing the wrong way?"

Yandika looked, but he could not see, and wondered if poor Mwami was imagining things. He was getting very old now, and senile; recently, on many occasions, he had seen or heard things no others had. Perhaps he had better humour the old chap.

"Well, yes — I suppose it is," he said, but as he spoke he realised Mwami was right, for out in midstream the smooth surface gently eddied in wide circles which moved, always, upriver.

There was nothing more to say. Neither of them possessed the intellectual power to work out any answer to the puzzle; it was completely outside their experience.

Another day passed and by then it was raining over the whole valley; a steady, soaking drizzle. Still the water rose, and the river continued to back slowly upstream.

Later, the high ground to which the impalas had moved became isolated, an island from which, if the waters did not fall, the only escape would be to swim. Few of them, except Kali-Anuka, who had received many swimming lessons from his father, would be willing to enter the water without persuasion.

But it was not necessary.

As though somewhere the pent-up waters had been released, the level began to fall, only slightly at first, but then in a steady, gurgling stream; and the danger had passed.

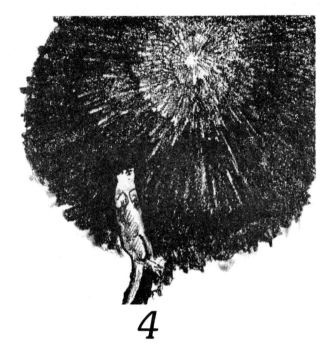

4

ALTHOUGH Tantalika always recognised the moment
when Fura-Uswa wished to communicate with him, he
never knew for certain whether he was awake or sleeping.

But his instructions were clear: before the fullness of the
moon of Muyobo, he was to go to the Big Rock, which lay on
the bed of the gorge, close to the Zimikile dam. There the
spirit of Nyaminyami dwelt, and there Fura-Uswa would be
awaiting him.

When the time came he went down into the gorge, dived
deep into the rushing waters and, battling strongly against the
current, reached the entrance hole in the bottom of the rock,
and up into the dry, hollow chamber. It was quite round, and
big enough for the largest river-snake to curl up in. Though he
could feel the presence of Nyaminyami, he never heard his

voice. Fura-Uswa was there, too; he knew this immediately, for high in the chamber hovered a tiny light, no bigger than a firefly's.

He waited, braced against the wall, his body shaped to its curve, his hind paws hard against the edge of the hole. At last, when his tail ached with cramp, the point of light slowly grew brighter until the chamber was flooded with a pure white radiance. He waited for Fura-Uswa to break the silence, twisting upright, and letting his tail hang down in the hole to relieve his cramp.

"Welcome, otter!"

It was a small voice, like the squeaky grunting of a mongoose, yet it filled the chamber overwhelmingly, echoing around the walls.

"I welcome you in great sorrow," began Fura-Uswa, "for I am now certain that those creatures you call the Zimikile are trying to destroy all the living things in the Great Valley, and even the valley itself. They began this fiendish plan many, many moons ago, slaying my own kind into eternal extinction. They have tried with others, but have not succeeded; now they have become impatient to destroy everything, without delay.

"I have tried to stop them, but alone I did not have the power. I can do much but not enough. Only Nyaminyami, the great River God (who is here but you cannot hear him) can bring down the forces from the sky, from under the earth, and from the air, to thwart the evil intent which crawls from men's hearts into their minds.

"Twelve moons past, Nyaminyami brought all the waters from the great waterfall that thunders, and the river flowed with such force that their mountain was swept away. But they ignored the warning, and re-created what had been destroyed. Now, he has tried again, as you saw with your own eyes. This time he pushed the waters down from all other rivers, too, and made the clouds heavier with rain than ever before. This time he has succeeded, this time they will, surely, heed the warning unless they are mad!"

By now Fura-Uswa's voice had pitched to a high,

shrieking scream. Tantalika's paws went up to cover his ears, but he knew this would anger the godkin, and he brought them down.

It was very quiet in the chamber, and when Fura-Uswa spoke again, his voice was so small that Tantalika could only just hear his words.

"This is what Nyaminyami believes," he said, "but I know the ways of men better than he. They will not give up easily." There was another long silence, and then Fura-Uswa said, in his normal voice: "Now, otter, tell me of what you have seen while roaming the Great Valley."

Tantalika spoke of the abandoned Zimikile villages, and the killing of animals, insects and trees. But he wondered if the godkin listened, for before he had finished, Fura-Uswa interrupted.

"If the Zimikile make another mountain across the gorge," he said, "it will be twice as strong as the one which now lies broken, under the river. Then, neither I nor Nyaminyami will be able to save the Great Valley, and it will drown under the Zimikile sea. All living things that can run, or crawl, or fly, or swim, must go as high and as far from the river as they can. We will know if this is to happen, for the moon of Nalupale will not be visible in the sky . . . that will be the omen, and all must take heed, at once.

"Then, otter, you must come to me again, but not here. You will come to the baobab trees, the place of Ma-buyu, where I will be spending next summer. There is too much water hereabouts; I do not care for it, and shall be glad to be gone."

The light in the chamber dimmed, and when it became a tiny, sparkling dot, as it had begun, Tantalika was just able to hear Fura-Uswa's final words.

"Now go, otter," he said in a thin whisper, "and go well!"

It was never very clear to Tantalika what transpired during his rare meetings with the godkin, and he always found it curious that afterwards, for several days, he would find himself remembering things that had happened, and the words that had been spoken, of which he had been unaware at the time.

Now, as he began his return journey, thoughts entered his mind which he knew were not his own, but those of Fura-Uswa, although he had no recollection of them having been spoken. They answered some of the riddles which had been bothering him ever since he had first known of the strange actions of the Zimikile in the valley. But, he decided, there was plenty of time to piece everything together to make a whole, which he could tell Mwami at the end of his long journey home.

But it took longer than he had intended. When the angry waters had piled up against the dam, the first sudden flood had lasted only briefly, but the river continued to flow, swift and swollen. Even he was not a strong enough swimmer to move for long against the force of the current. The river was, over some stretches, five times wider than normal, and with all its many tributaries rushing down, overflowing, to join the mainstream, he was forced to make a detour for long distances southwards where the floods had not reached. If they had, he was able to keep to high ground, occasionally having to cross water which cut through the valleys. But this suited him well, for he met with many impala herds who had pulled back from the floods, and he told them the reason for the floods, regretting he could not reach those who dwelt in the north.

He had just swum across one of these valley stretches, walking sometimes on the shallow bed, and was crawling out on to a smooth rock when he sniffed the pleasant scent of otter. He whistled, and scrambled over the rock towards a broken kopje, following the scent with growing excitement. He heard an answering whistle, and an overwhelming warmth filled his heart.

Sitting on a boulder, a small she-otter waited for him. He did not speak to her as he came up, keeping his distance, until she gave a little flick of her tail. Then he chirped at her, moved closer, put his forepaws on the stone and looked up into her face. He chirped again, reaching up to touch her nose with his, then licked her face. She continued to ignore him, so he whimpered impatiently and bit her ear. She slid off the rock, down into the water and with a playful, inviting sweep of her rudder swam away.

He followed her, swimming more strongly than she, until they swam side by side; then they rolled and splashed happily in the shallow water, stirring up the red mud. Soon they tired of the game and together, on shore again, they searched under stones for insect larvae.

Her name was Vutuka, because of the white blaze between her eyes, and Tantalika fell in love with her. She was much younger than he, only in her second year, and had been alone since her mother had died in a wire snare set by two young poachers soon after she was weaned. That she had survived for so long, fending for herself, was remarkable, and this endeared her greatly to Tantalika. He was gentle with her, for she seemed a little frightened of him, so that he dreaded doing anything to drive her away. But after a few days together she lost her fear, and although it was too late in the season to take her as his mate, she returned his love in the only way she could, by swimming off, frequently, and bringing him gifts of fish.

In his ecstasy at finding her at last, Tantalika temporarily forgot about the impalas, the dam and Fura-Uswa; he forgot about the life-threat to the valley which, before, had been uppermost in his mind. So for many days they hunted and played together, sleeping where they had met at the kopje, in a crevice among the boulders. But when the floodwaters had drained off, and they had to seek fishing grounds at greater distances, Tantalika began to pine for his old bachelor haunts, and they set off one day for Mwami's country, far to the south-west.

On the way they passed many places where the Zimikile had cleared the trees and bush, and when they neared the river all traces of Batonka villages had gone, swept to extinction by the floods. None had been rebuilt, as though the people did not intend to return.

Tantalika visited many more impala herds, conveying Fura-Uswa's message to them. It was vague and garbled, but they were able to grasp something of the meaning which lay behind the recent events in the valley, and were forewarned of possible new trials to come.

Early one evening, the two otters had been diving for fish in a quiet little creek, and each with a victim held in the mouth, were racing to the shore when Vutuka, who was ahead, suddenly dived. While she was still under, Tantalika saw a crocodile sliding through the water in her direction. Its craggy nostrils and eyes were visible, and although it moved so silently only a slight ripple disturbed the surface. Tantalika dived too, trying to catch up with Vutuka to warn her of the danger, but he was too late and saw, through the underwater gloom, her lithe body shoot upwards. There were sharp, confused movements, and the water seemed to boil when the croc snapped at her tail with its massive jaws. Coming up under the croc's belly, he diverted its attention from her, and it twisted round to snap at his head. But Tantalika was too quick, coiling his body so that his short front legs were positioned to poke his fingers into both eyes of his adversary, who hissed in frustration and pain. The powerful tail swung round and slapped at the otter, but missed, sending up a spray of water. Nimbly, Tantalika jerked himself on to the croc's head, held on by his hind legs for dear life while he gouged his fingers deeper into the croc's eye-sockets. Thrashing about, trying to dislodge the little otter, the croc, with a desperate effort and spurred by the pain, threw its head upwards and sideways. Tantalika was dislodged so successfully that he was thrown far enough for a head-start in his streak to the cluster of reeds near the shore. He splashed through them, pulled himself up on to the bank and collapsed across a dead tree trunk, well out of harm's way. He watched through half-closed eyes as the thwarted, sore-eyed crocodile cut through the water towards the opposite bank.

He looked for Vutuka, but could not see her. For a long time he lay on the tree, all his senses alert for some sign of her. It was twilight before she darted up out of the water in front of him, a large fish clamped in her jaws for both to share. He admonished her for going back into the water, but he felt closer to her than ever before, and she to him.

In the morning they moved away from the creek, for where there is one crocodile there are usually more. They set off once again upstream, but it was many days before they reached the territory of the Pambuka. By then the river had calmed to the languid flow of winter months, for almost a whole year had passed since the otter had first set forth on his travels.

Kali-Anuka and Kusomona had also been developing a close bond. Neither had reached full maturity, and certainly their mothers still treated them as juveniles, not yet permitting them to stay out of sight for more than a few moments. Mwami himself would not normally allow this even of mature impalas, jealously guarding his herd, fearful not only of the dangers which could threaten a single, isolated individual, but also of the possibility of trespass into alien territory, which is contrary to the social laws of the impala species.

It was a very dark night when Kali-Anuka and Kusomona wandered too far away and very nearly came to grief. The darkness had fallen when Mwami carefully led his charges to a new resting-place he had discovered, a little further away from the river than the normal one. The stars were invisible behind an overcast sky, which seemed to press down heavily over the parched woodland, holding the still, sun-warmed air from the day close to the ground. The two youngsters trailed behind their mothers, chasing each other in the darkness, but always within scenting distance of the herd. Then, at one moment as they ran into a clump of thorn bushes, Kusomona heard a sound above her head, a 'click-click' so close that she jumped in alarm, and fell against her companion. Before they knew what had happened the dry, cracked ground gave way beneath them and they fell, in a flurry of dust and kicking hooves, down the steep slope of an eroded gully.

"What scared you?" asked Kali-Anuka, as they scrambled to their feet.

Her little voice trembled.

"Just an owl, I think," she said. "But it was so close and loud!"

They laughed together in a burst of short snorts, and turned to climb up from the bed of the donga. But it was too steep, and all their sharp little hooves did was to dislodge more and more of the loose soil.

"Come on," ordered Kali-Anuka, "let's try somewhere else."

They shook the dust off their coats and walked together, Kali-Anuka leading, along the rough floor of the gully. The further they went, the narrower it became and its sides higher and steeper. No animal can see in complete darkness, and down here not a glimmer of light penetrated from the cloud-masked sky above; the only thing to do was to turn back and seek a way out at the other end.

They reached the starting place and both lifted their heads high, calling and snorting as loud as they could. Kali-Anuka even managed an immature roar; but it was no use, and none heard. They went on, but it was a long time before the donga broadened out and the sides became less steep. And then, with blessed relief, they were able to gain faltering footholds with Kali-Anuka helping his friend by shoving at her rump with his head.

Once at the top they laughed at their adventure, then considered the next move, for they both knew they were now far from the herd.

Kusomona was apprehensive.

"Don't worry," said Kali-Anuka, "we just need to follow the edge of the donga — and make sure we don't fall into it again!"

They went, and although they could see only the vague shapes of trees and bushes and rocks looming up close in the blackness, they found where they had fallen. But there was no sound or scent of the other impalas.

Kusomona, now on the edge of panic, trotted away from the acacias, calling her mother.

"Mawe!" she cried, "maaa-weee! . . . are you there?"

But her soft voice did not carry far and, as if mocking her, an owl hooted from high in a tree as she passed beneath it, and there was the whisper of its downy wings as it flew close above her head. She ducked instinctively, then fell back to be beside Kali-Anuka.

"Oh Kali — I'm so frightened!" she murmured.

Comforting her, he licked and nuzzled her face and neck. They stood still for a moment, and he could feel her body shiver against his, not with cold, but with fear.

They found, at the foot of a precipitous kopje, an overhang of rock forming an open cave. Nothing, except perhaps a venomous snake, could attack them from above without warning, and they lay there all night, snatching short moments of sleep until, gradually, the woodland shapes took on recognisable forms as the rising sun tinged the sky a pale pink.

Kali-Anuka waited, head raised high and nostrils quivering as he tried to pick up the scent of impalas, but there were so many other animal smells on the air he was unable to separate them. Then, as full daylight suffused the sky, he smelt the river, and knew what direction they should take.

"We must go like the wind," he said. "Keep close behind me, and keep going — whatever happens!"

They went, each in a swift, diving rush, zigzagging in great leaps, airborne over bushes and boulders, plunging on towards the river. Birds flew up from the ground, and off low branches, scattering before them in twittering panic. A family of warthogs, busy rooting out rhizomes, galloped away squealing, with tails erect. A lone zebra, fooled into a desperate bid for self-preservation, tossed his mane and fled behind them, certain that a cheetah, at least, was at his heels.

Leaping over a straggling flame acacia, Kali-Anuka landed beside a peacefully ruminating Mwami. Kusomona followed, nearly impaling herself on his horns; then came the astonished zebra. Jumping up, Mwami roared, and the rest of the herd swirled round uncertainly until all were in full flight from their non-existent attackers.

There is only one form of serious punishment for an impala, and that is banishment from the herd. But Kali-Anuka and Kusomona were too young for such a severe sentence, and got away with hard, mature advice from Mwami, and a mild scolding from their mothers.

And for all they knew, the zebra kept running.

It was night, with the cold, white moon of Gandapati riding high, and all the stars of the heavens flashing like diamonds. Under the silvery brightness, in a clearing near the edge of some woodland, the herd of impala rested, the only sounds an occasional sharp tap of a hoof on rock, a muted snort, or, if one listened closely, the steady munching of dry browse. Not far away the river gurgled sluggishly, and across the water came the low, regular "hurruhm . . . hurruhm . . . hurruhm . . ." from a young lioness. A hyena barked; there was a sudden crescendo from chittering monkeys, a hollow bird call, and then all was quiet again, except for the rustle of brittle leaves in the night breeze.

Under a solitary buffalo-thorn tree which grew out of an old termite mound, a group of four impalas listened to an otter telling a story, and only one impala, the wise old Mwami, found it difficult to believe all Tantalika said. It was not that he thought him a liar — that is a word unknown to any section of the animal world — but he had known the otter long enough to treat with suspicion some of his extravagant talk, never quite sure where a reasonable balance between fact and fantasy could be found. But perhaps it did not matter, really, so long as no harm was done and no impalas were misled on important matters. The others listened spellbound, and Vutuka, a little shy among her strange new friends, hung on every word, understanding none. She lay, fully stretched, beside Tantalika, her chin resting comfortably on the thickest part of his tail. Half-reclining, Mwami sat, flanked by Yandika and Kali-Anuka; the only doe in the audience was Swilila, who rested with her legs tucked under her belly, ruminating thoughtfully throughout the otter's story.

It was Mwami who interrupted the non-stop flow of words, when Tantalika had described, vividly, his entrance into the Big Rock, and the round chamber within it.

"Tell me," he said, "how do other animals manage when they go to the Big Rock, as they must do, sometimes?" He did not wish to embarrass the otter, but he felt the others were owed an explanation. "An elephant, for example. Or a buffalo. Few animals cannot swim, after a fashion, but very few I know of can swim underwater."

Tantalika scratched his head between his ears.

"M'm," he said. "I've never thought of that . . . I'll ask Fura-Uswa next time I go to him."

Mwami shook his head, and smiled with his eyes.

The otter quickly resumed, remembering everything Fura-Uswa had said, and more besides. He was quoting the godkin's prediction that the Zimikile would not give up easily, when a snore from the now sleeping Vutuka brought giggling snorts from Yandika, cut off by a muted one from Kali-Anuka.

"Listen!" he said urgently.

Four pairs of impala ears came forward, and Mwami climbed to his hooves. Tantalika pointed his nose upwards, sniffing the night air. All their senses were straining. But except for a breeze whispering through the trees, and the calls of night birds above the shrill vibrations of cicadas, there were no unusual sounds.

"I hear nothing," said Mwami, but despite himself he spoke quietly. "What was it, Kali-Anuka?"

"A carrier-creature . . . far away," Kali-Anuka said, with certainty.

"I can't hear it," said Tantalika, sniffing between the words. "But I can smell it, and I should know about . . ."

"There it is again! Listen . . ."

They could all hear it now, and smell it, too. But the sound came in waves, rising and falling in intensity.

Mwami was the first to relax, and lowered himself to the ground once more.

"The nearest Zimikile trail is far, far away," he said with confidence. "It is a trick of the wind that we can hear and smell it at such a distance. Come, Tantalika — continue your story, for dawn will soon be here and we will have to move away."

Vutuka, disturbed from sleep, settled down again with her head on Tantalika's tail; the impalas, stimulated by the minor diversion, waited for the continuation of the entertainment. But Kali-Anuka remained more sharply alert than the others.

"Now you will want to know why the Zimikile have been doing such strange things all over the Great Valley," Tantalika went on, and the impalas nodded eagerly, although Mwami wondered what the otter could possibly think up next. "I reported on all the sights I had seen, but Fura-Uswa already knew of them, and told me they are because the sharp-faced, pale Zimikile want to stop the river with their dam, so that the valley will flood into a great sea, which they would rather have than what is here now. But if the dark people are not moved away they will all drown; many trees must die for them, so that they have ground on which to grow their food. Insects have to die, although there is only one they are frightened of: the inguluzi which bites and sickens to a sleeping death. And because this fly feeds on the blood of so many animals, they too must die."

"And birds?" Swilila asked quietly. "I hear many birds are dying, too."

Tantalika inclined his head, and gazed into the dark foliage of the branches above him.

"Of what use are the birds . . . to these Zimikile?" he asked.

In the pause that followed, Kali-Anuka listened for the sound he had heard before; but there was nothing, although the faint scent of a carrier-creature was still in his nostrils.

"The really important message I have from Fura-Uswa," Tantalika said pompously, "is this: should the Zimikile make another dam, it will be twice as strong as the last. Then, neither he nor Nyaminyami will be able to save the Great Valley. All living things will have to go far away from the river; we will be warned of this should the moon of Nalupale be invisible in the sky."

"Will *you* go?" asked Kali-Anuka.

"We'll see, when — if — the time comes."

To the east, the sky lightened along the horizon, and, hastening to finish his story, Tantalika accounted for his journey home, and of all he had seen and done; but he did not dwell long on his meeting with Vutuka. When he had done, there was a long silence, partly because Mwami had fallen asleep, and Vutuka's snoring had ceased.

Once more, it was Kali-Anuka who asked a question.

"You have told us this mountain across the river — this dam, as you call it — will cause the whole of the Great Valley to flood, if the Zimikile have their way. I can understand that. But I cannot understand *why* they wish to do this? For what purpose? Surely *they* do not want to store fish, or make a great pool for their young to play in, like your friends from far away?"

Tantalika was nonplussed. He could think of no answer to this, not even one he could invent.

"There must be a reason, Kali-Anuka . . . but I don't know what it is," he admitted lamely.

"Does Fura-Uswa not know, either? Does perhaps Nya-minyami know, but has not told the godkin?" There was a note of sarcasm in Kali-Anuka's voice, but it was lost on the otter.

"All I can do is to ask him," said Tantalika.

It was not only because he wanted to escape from more questioning that Tantalika suddenly moved a couple of short paces forward, so that Vutuka's bristly chin thumped to the ground under his tail. She awoke with a start and, at a sign from her mate, both otters ran off towards the river to begin their normal activities of the day, for by now the starlight had flickered and died as the sun crept up towards the distant skyline.

For the impalas, having rested inactive for much of the night, there was an immediate urge to feed, and they moved off to join the rest of the herd among the trees. Mwami lingered behind and, feeling the need to relieve himself, paused for the purpose at the midden — the communal dung heap.

He stood with his hindquarters towards a spreading fig tree, and an early-rising oxpecker flew down on to his shoulder in search of ticks. His business completed, Mwami was about to move off when the tick-bird suddenly flew up with its rattling, warning cry. At the same moment the old impala heard the sharp crack of the bullet from the rifle, and felt the scorching pain as the red-hot lead pierced his flank. He tried to leap away, but the springing power had gone from a hind leg, and he crumpled to the ground, his blunted horn shattering against a rock. He managed a warning roar but the herd had already run off at the sound of the shot, to seek safety deeper among the trees. Only Kali-Anuka and Yandika remained, standing together still and alert, in the middle of the clearing.

There was another shot, closer to Mwami this time, but

the bullet missed, ricocheting off the rock under the ram's remaining horn, whining away through the air, dropping uselessly in a small explosion of earth. Breathing heavily from shock Mwami saw the blood oozing from the wound, down his leg, and then looked up into the pale face of the hunter, a few paces from him. Slightly to one side was another, dark-faced and with a rifle slung across his shoulder.

Gathering all his remaining strength, unsure whether to attempt flight or, uncharacteristically for an impala, to fight back, Mwami heaved himself painfully up on his legs, twisting round so that he faced his adversaries. Two rifles were raised and pointed at him as he snorted his defiance, and lowered his single horn. He swayed a little, recovered, and thrust forward at the two men.

A sudden staccato clopping of hooves on hard ground, and a brushing of undergrowth, made the two men turn away, startled. Mwami's horn, held as low as he could, with his full weight behind it, pierced the white man's stomach, and as he fell, the impala's sharp hooves split his face from ear to chin.

The other fired aimlessly at Kali-Anuka and Yandika who were leaping towards him. Mwami, carried on by his own momentum, stumbled, and zigzagged drunkenly through the bush with blind, unconscious instinct, unaware that he had got his man. The wounded victim screamed with pain as his companion ran to him, once he saw the two young rams had veered off to follow Mwami into the bush.

They found him quickly, lying on his side in the middle of a little clearing, his beautiful coat dulled, the white lower parts streaked with blood, already drying except where it flowed from his deep wound.

He was alive, but clinging to his last moments as all creatures do when close to death.

Kali-Anuka and Yandika stood over him, heads lowered, licking away the blood. The old ram spoke with an effort, his voice softer than usual.

"Kali-Anuka," he said, "do not believe all the otter says, but heed him. Before Yandika, I am bequeathing you the leadership of the Pambuka . . . you may be challenged, but do not fail me. Only you . . . " here he faltered, struggling with his last words, ". . . only you can save my Pambuka . . . from what . . . may come. Ko caala, my son . . . ko caala . . ."

His voice faded altogether as the old ram died.

"Ka sike, Mwami!" Kali-Anuka murmured, and Yandika echoed his farewell.

Although there was still the scent of man — and man's blood — on the air for a long time, the hunters were not seen again. But later that morning, all the Pambuka heard the distant sound of a carrier-creature; and it grew fainter and fainter until they could hear it no more.

5

SOON it was rutting time again, and the mature rams fought over the ripe does. Wherever impalas ranged in the Great Valley, there came the clashing of horns and those strange, turkey-gobble roars and sibilant snorts which are peculiar to them at this season.

Kali-Anuka was challenged neither for his leadership, nor for his possession of Kusomona, and for almost half a year a peace descended over the herd, and they wished it could last for ever. Their lives drifted by gently, with food plentiful after two seasons of heavy rains and floods. There were few unpleasant incidents to remember; and Kusomona's smooth white belly filled out with her unborn lamb.

Nothing was seen or heard of Tantalika, nor Vutuka, until the first tentative rains began. Then he suddenly appeared amid the herd at the river beach one damply oppressive afternoon. He ran about calling for Mwami, but it was not until he found Kali-Anuka that he received the news of the old ram's death.

"Why do you rush about, calling for Mwami, when he has been gone for six moons?" asked Kali-Anuka.

The otter stood erect, and leaned against a rock, taken aback at his friend's words.

"Gone?" he said. "Gone where?"

"His bones lie close by, and sometimes I think his spirit still lives with us. Our Mwami is dead, Tantalika, struck down by the noise from a Zimikile stick." His voice was bitter.

"I did not know. Truly, I did not know."

"But you're supposed to know all things. Does the spirit of Fura-Uswa no longer converse with you?"

"Yes, yes — of course. But it is unlikely he would be aware of such a small matter —"

"A *small* matter?" Kali-Anuka tossed his head contemptuously. "You call Mwami's death a *small* matter? He, who once saved your life, he who was loved and respected by us all — by all impalas of the Great Valley? You disappoint me, my friend."

"I didn't mean it in the way you think, Kali-Anuka. Nor do *I* regard such a loss as of no consequence. But to Fura-Uswa it can be of little significance, for many, many animals and birds die every day in his great domain. You understand that, don't you?" he added, almost pleadingly.

"I understand only that you're an ungrateful otter, when I'd hoped the friendship you had for poor Mwami, and the debt you owe him would continue with me, as his successor, and the others of the Pambuka."

"But it does!" insisted Tantalika. Then, as Kali-Anuka turned away from him, he dropped on all fours and said angrily: "I'll show you how much, Kali-Anuka:"

His fur bristled defiantly, his whiskers twitched, and he ran off into the river, swimming back to his holt on the far bank.

The news of Mwami's death affected him profoundly. Although his friendship with young Kali-Anuka was strong, it had not as yet had the chance of developing to the deep trust, the respect he had held for Mwami. It would come, he hoped, but this had been a bad start. He was understanding enough to realise why his unthinking remark had upset Kali-Anuka, but he remained cross and in a black mood which was not helped by the absence of Vutuka. She had gone off the day before on some private expedition of her own, and he did not expect her to return until Maziba, the first month of the new year, which is the mating time for otters.

In self-imposed solitude, he hid himself away in the hollow under the river bank; this was out of character, for usually during the summer months he preferred to roam day and night revelling in the rain and dampness, snatching brief sleep wherever he happened to be.

Now, he did not venture outside except to feed, and as the days passed, his boredom grew with his inactivity. But one evening, when he judged the moon of Nalupale to be near to fullness, he eagerly emerged from his holt, though his heart was filled with foreboding as he cleaved upwards through the water. He broke surface, shook the water from his eyes, and looked up to the sky as he made for the shore. He scrambled, his little heart singing, on to a rocky ledge which thrust out above the water. He lay there, bathed in the silvery light from the star-scattered sky and his own happiness, watching the high horizon as it was slowly steeped in a band of light from the rising moon. As the light grew in intensity, so his heart lifted even more.

But then the tip of a dark cloud, white-fringed, heaved up over the uneven skyline, and grew bigger; the moon came with it, behind, and invisible. Appalled, Tantalika stretched up on his hind legs, as though by doing so he could see over the cloud, which rose up along the horizon, the white edges darkening rapidly. The light from the moon faded, and the great, unbroken mass rolled up and over the valley, a huge, sliding canopy. Then the rain came down, hot and grey, and Tantalika slipped off the rock, to swim slowly and miserably back to his holt.

For the rest of that night he remained there, scratching idly at the earth floor with his little fingers, pondering deeply, picturing the terrible flood to come. He was not concerned about his own fate, for he above all animals was best equipped to cope with it.

The rain was still falling, but softly now, when he crossed the river soon after dawn. He found Kali-Anuka lying alone, ruminating, under a big waterberry tree, and came up to him quietly, from behind.

"I just nosed in for a chat," he said with forced cheerfulness, noting that Kali-Anuka did not even start at the sound of his voice.

"Wa buka, Tantalika," Kali-Anuka greeted, coldly, and continued chewing.

The otter went straight to the point of his visit.

"Kali-Anuka," he said firmly, "I am sorry I lost my temper with you the other day. Before that I did not know I had one, but poor Mwami's death upset me very much, and I did not think how — er, any impala could possibly take his place." He hurried on without a pause. "But I know now I was very wrong and should encourage you, not, as I did in my thoughts, condemn you so soon after you took his place. We *must* remain friends — close friends — for the sake of all the Pambuka, and all other impalas. Specially now," he added solemnly, "when so much danger threatens."

Kali-Anuka had not interrupted this little speech, nor did he say anything for a few moments after it.

Then, swallowing the last lump of cud, he dipped his head in acceptance of Tantalika's apology.

"I agree, Tantalika, and I was to blame as much as you. Mwami would have wished us to remain close, and to be angry with you is to be angry with, ahem — Fura-Uswa. Now," he said quietly, "tell me what new danger threatens."

"It is the danger I spoke of before Mwami died. Last night it was the moon of Nalupale — not quite full, for as you know, all strange happenings and witchery are squeezed into that last portion. But the moon could not be seen, because of the storm clouds, and this was the sign that the Zimikile have rebuilt their dam. Soon the river will rise, and go on rising until the whole valley drowns beneath it."

At first, as he remembered Mwami's dying words, Kali-Anuka was not perturbed overmuch with the otter's news.

"When will this happen?" he asked, calmly.

"That I don't know. It could begin soon. I will have to go to the place of Ma-buyu, and Fura-Uswa will tell me."

"Do you know where this place is?"

The otter hesitated.

"Well, er — yes, I think so. In fact, I'm quite sure, and it is across the river, far to the north." He hesitated again, not sure of how much he should tell the impala. Then: "Last night came the strange sensation I feel whenever Fura-Uswa wishes to communicate with me." He groped for a way of expressing himself, so that Kali-Anuka would understand. "His voice cannot be heard at these times," he went on, "but pictures form deep in my mind, and with them, I am guided to the meeting place, or wherever he wants me to go."

Kali-Anuka pondered these words, half-believing them, but still he remained sceptical. There was really, he decided at last, only one way to find out the truth, once and for all. He scrambled to his hooves, and shook himself.

"I'll come with you, Tantalika," he said firmly. "We'll go together to this place you call Ma-buyu."

The otter stared at him in disbelief. He did not want the impala to go with him to share in that mystical connection with Fura-Uswa, which was a tenuous thread, easily broken if he incurred the displeasure of the godkin. But he could not say this, knowing that Kali-Anuka's scepticism would be reinforced.

"You cannot go with me," he objected, "for I know you impalas are poor swimmers, and the river is too wide for you to cross."

Kali-Anuka smiled, his eyes softening.

"Do you forget who my father was?" he asked. "When I

was very young, Mwami taught me to swim better than any of our kind, and twice we crossed the river together, and back again. It was not difficult, although we had to watch out for crocodiles."

The otter tried once more.

"I don't know what Fura-Uswa will say to this," he said, guardedly. "He may be very angry."

"Well, let's go and find out, shall we, Tantalika?"

Kali-Anuka appointed Yandika as temporary leader during his absence. He told none the reason for his journey, except Yandika and Swilila, for others did not need to know. He begged Swilila and Silulimi to watch over Kusomona, and the birth of his offspring should it occur while he was away.

So, when all had been arranged, the otter and the impala went down to the familiar beach, and side by side splashed into the shallows, beginning their extraordinary trek to a place that one of them suspected did not exist.

They swam across the broad river without mishap. Quickly outdistancing the impala, Tantalika slid up on to the ledge of rock where, the night before, he had sat watching for the moon. Kali-Anuka's hooves squelched in the mud under the reeds, and he hauled himself up beside the otter; he stood quietly for a long time, breathing heavily after his great exertions, unable to speak.

"You did very well," said Tantalika. "Very praiseworthy — for an impala!"

Kali-Anuka snorted, but still he could not speak.

"A bit slow," the otter said, critically, and fingered his moustache. "If you grew a tail like mine, instead of that rabbit stub, you'd do better!" He chuckled at his little joke, snapping his teeth together several times.

When Kali-Anuka had rested, they moved upstream, keeping close to the river except where the tangled undergrowth forced them to strike inland for short distances. Although it was still early morning, the heat lay heavy, in slow-moving wraiths of mist carried along by the languid river flow, not yet hastened with the torrential rains to come. After the storm of the previous night, water dripped from the trees, and the ground was soft and slippery where the winter dust had mingled with the first showers to a smooth paste. Often, Kali-Anuka nearly fell as his hooves slithered in the thick mud.

By late morning, they reached a tumble of big boulders, forming a low kopje which jutted out from the bank and seemed, at first glance, to be an island, but a narrow strip of sand connected it to the shore. Without hesitation the otter turned away from it, northwards, with his companion following, unquestioning, in his path. They did not go far, for Kali-Anuka was weakening quickly, and called for a rest; the swim across the river had taxed his strength more than he cared to admit.

They rested under the shade of a big marula tree which, in early winter, would bear the acid-sweet fruits so much relished by many wild animals of Africa, who sometimes became intoxicated from eating fermented fruit lying on the ground. Kali-Anuka ate the fallen, waxy-white flowers from a your. baobab nearby; he lay down, his rubbery mouth working as he munched in his sleep.

Ever active, his reserves of energy seldom used to the full, Tantalika rested only briefly before he returned to the island kopje to scratch for tiny crabs under the small boulders which littered the water's edge. He thought no more of his efforts to dissuade Kali-Anuka from accompanying him to Ma-buyu, but put his mind to cracking the shells of the crabs he caught, one by one, against a rock, stuffing the sweet-tasting meat into his mouth with his usual gusto.

His hunger satisfied, and Kali-Anuka on his feet again ready to continue the journey, the otter did not hesitate to lead the way northwards, crossing many small streams and sandy pools, patterned over a wide, softly rolling plain which spread below the foothills of a low escarpment.

Soon the afternoon heat, the long, slow climb ever higher over the foothills towards the summit of the escarpment, began to tell on the limits of the impala's endurance. They rested again, Kali-Anuka deciding that contrary to whatever the otter may wish, they would remain here until next morning.

There was a little waterfall nearby, tumbling down from a ledge into a broad pool, the bed worn deep under the fall by centuries of erosion, but elsewhere silted up with sand. Further down, the pool narrowed into a stream which gurgled over a bed of stones, to disappear under a dense overhanging tangle of rose-flowered wild gentian. This little sanctuary was coolly shaded by a grove of low-branched waterberry trees and, except for the trickling stream and wind-whispering of the trees, it was quiet — even the birds were resting.

Kali-Anuka found plenty to eat: fresh green grasses, leaves, and the fleshy, acid fruit of the waterberries. The otter had to work harder, in the deepest part of the pool, scooping small fish into his mouth, finding none bigger than the length of his fingers. After drinking, they both settled down to rest through to the evening, Tantalika stretched out along a cool

slab of rock, lightly washed
by the running stream, his
tail dangling in the water;
the impala half-lying, with
his head up, almost hidden
among the reeds which grew
close to the waterfall.

Late in the afternoon,
a small herd of elephants
threaded through the trees along a well-worn trail, their
stomachs rumbling. In single file on their heavy, soft-soled
feet, heads nodding rhythmically, trunks swinging, they
plodded on silently towards the pool. Two calves, thinly
trumpeting, ran to keep up with their mothers.

The leading elephant, a big cow well past her prime,
paused a little way from the edge of the pool, and as though
this was a signal to the others, they gathered in a group
behind her, standing close. The tip of the old cow's trunk
brushed lightly over the ground, scenting suspiciously; then
it swung high, waving from side to side, analysing the scents
carried on the wind. Her great ears, unfurled, spreading like
a pair of broad wings; satisfied, she relaxed and slowly walked
to the water. Before she reached it, she was overtaken by one
of the calves, who splashed eagerly into the shallows, squealing
with delight.

The noise awakened Tantalika, who instantly slipped off
his rock into the pool, unaware of what had alarmed him.
Playing safe, he swam underwater until he had to come up for
air, and when he did, the old female, who had just sucked up
a stream of water, squirted it full in the otter's face.

There was a great blast of trumpeting from the elephants,
and the trees around shook to their roots from the laughter.
Tantalika, spluttering for air, fur bristling with anger, swam
away and crawled over the sand to join Kali-Anuka, who stood
quietly, his eyes hiding a smile.

"That wasn't a nice thing to do," said Tantalika grumpily.
"Quite unnecessary, in fact." He glared across at the elephants,
now enjoying their drinking and bathing, their little joke
already forgotten. The otter did not stay by the pool, but
wandered off in search of a more peaceful spot.

Soon there was a large gathering of animals scattered round the pool. A pair of sable bulls drank side by side with a family of warthogs; a group of grysbok shared the stream with a dozen robust buffalo; zebras, duikers, impalas and water-buck crowded round, drinking, all nervously alert for any unusual sound, scent or movement.

Kali-Anuka felt a soft, wet nudge against his shoulder. He flinched, but it was only the nose of another impala ram, who had spotted the stranger standing there alone.

"Nduwe ni? Who are you?" asked the ram. "I have not seen you here before, have I?"

"The answer to your second question is – no. To the first question I answer – I am Kali-Anuka, the leader of the Pambuka herd from across the river."

The other pondered this before he spoke again, and there was more respect in his voice.

"Wa buka, Kali-Anuka. But — forgive me if I doubt you — isn't the honoured Mwami your leader?"

"Mwami is dead. Hadn't you heard?"

"We have little news of events in the Great Valley. I believe there is some strange animal who should keep us informed, a messenger from Fura-Uswa, the godkin I was told about when I was very young. But I haven't led my herd for long, and know little of these things. I'm sorry to learn of Mwami's death — all of us know of him. But tell me, Kali-Anuka, why are you, of the Pambuka, here — on the wrong side of the river?"

"There's no wrong side, my friend," answered Kali-Anuka. "The river and the Great Valley on either side of it belong to us all. I'm not sure, however, that this happy state of affairs will continue for very much longer."

The ram lifted a hind hoof to scratch under his chin.

"Oh?" he said, "why do you say such a thing?"

"Come with me and we'll talk to Tantalika, the otter."

His name was Kwizima, this stranger from another herd, so-called because his intelligence was rated quite high. He had proved this recently when, more by cunning than by physical strength, he had overcome three adversaries, and taken the leadership of his large herd.

"What kind of creature is *that?*" he asked as Tantalika, responding to Kali-Anuka's call, warily emerged from an empty warthog hole. "It looks like an oversize mongoose!"

Tantalika balanced on his hind legs, and drew himself up to his full height, so that his eyes met those of the questioner.

"I am an otter. But if we are to engage in any kind of conversation, you may call me Tantalika."

"Wa buka, Tantalika. And you may call me Kwizima. But tell me" — the impala tapped a front hoof, puzzled, — "how is it that a — an, er — otter, speaks in impala language?"

"The great Mwami, of the Pambuka, taught me." The otter tilted his head to one side, quizzically. "Who taught you, Kwizima, for I find it hard to understand your words?"

Kwizima snorted, amused.

"We are the impala of the north," he explained, "and

therefore our words may sound a little different, as do those of the south and other parts of the valley to us."

"Ah yes, of course. I've found this difficulty before when I've talked with your kind. Those who live far to the west I cannot understand at all."

Kwizima realised, then, who Tantalika was.

"Tell me," he said, "Kali-Anuka has spoken words of foreboding to me. What do you know of this?"

"I know enough, and it is true," Tantalika affirmed. He dropped to his paws, his feeling of antagonism towards the stranger evaporating. "The valley is to disappear under a great flood, and unless all animals move far, far away, they will all drown."

"When will this happen?"

"I don't know. Kali-Anuka and I have undertaken this journey to find out. But happen it will — you can be sure of that. I'm sorry not to have told you before, but I haven't known of it for long myself . . . and I've been rather busy."

Tantalika did not want to elaborate further; he did not wish to talk about Fura-Uswa, or the Zimikile dam. It was all too complicated, and he felt there would be little chance of an impala from a strange herd understanding much of it. He had given his warning, and it was up to this Kwizima whether or not he did anything about it. His duty was done, just as it had been done many times before, and it was only ever to the Pambuka he gave the full facts.

He need not have been concerned. Kwizima turned to Kali-Anuka, who had remained a silent listener throughout the conversation.

"Do you believe this ?"

Kali-Anuka hesitated before replying.

"I will tell you after we have completed our journey," he said.

"H'm." Kwizima asked no more questions. "So be it," he said. "Always our lives are as uncertain as a morning mist — they are there, they are gone. I, and each member of my herd, will meet this flood you talk of, should it come, just as we meet every flood, every year, or any other threat to our existence. But I will be obliged if, when you pass this way on your return from wherever you are going, you will tell me a little more of what we can expect, and when."

"Of course," agreed Tantalika.

"We will find you here?" Kali-Anuka asked.

"Invariably. But if not, because of bad weather, or some other reason which will be clear to you, we are never far away. Ko caala, Tantalika . . . ko caala, Kali-Anuka!" With a toss of his horned head, Kwizima leapt away to rejoin his herd down by the stream, leaving the others silent for a few moments.

When he spoke again, Tantalika said, almost to himself:

"I liked him, in the end. I hope we'll meet him again."

A son was born to Kusomona that night, and just as his father had entered the world to the music of thunder and the flashing of lightning, so did he.

It is unusual for an impala doe to give birth after sunset, or at any time during the hours of darkness, and Kusomona's instinct told her, as the brassy sun fell behind the storm-clouds gathering about the valley, that she must take extra care now that predators were becoming active. Restless and uncomfortable with early birth pains, a little bewildered, she wandered about, searching for Swilila and her own mother, Silulimi. She found them at last, just as the first rumble of thunder reverberated around the hills, and heavy drops of rain splashed noisily among the branches of the sheltering trees setting the leaves a-dancing. The storm grumbled about the darkening sky with no dramatic display of its anger, and the rain went on falling steadily while Kusomona, still restless, constantly shifted her position, standing, lying, then standing again. Swilila and Silulimi stayed close to her; there was no need for talk, but their presence was comforting.

She lay quietly at last, hardly conscious of her own efforts, and quite oblivious of her surroundings; she did not realise, for some time afterwards, that her lamb lay beside her, shaking his head and ears to clear them of moisture.

Then she looked back, surprised and alarmed, stared at her baby, sniffing towards him with ears pricked forward and eyes wide. Her alarm quickly changed to fascination. She cleaned herself while the lamb struggled to stand, his hind legs still hindered by the membranes enclosing them. Then, seeing he needed help, she started to lick him clean.

The rain pattered down, and the thunder rolled away on huge, lightning-lit clouds. Except for the calls of night-birds, and the hunting roars and barks of animal hunters far away, no sounds disturbed the start of the life of Mwami-Mupati, son of a leader, and nothing happened to delay the establishment of a strong bond between mother and young, so essential to the survival of any new-born animal in the free but dangerous world of the wild.

The grandmother does remained close to Kusomona and her suckling lamb all night, and in the morning, during that strange, silent limbo before sunrise when even the birds and cicadas are quiet, all four impalas walked together to mingle with the others, little Mupati stepping unsurely beside his mother, his eyes big with all the wonders they saw.

6

THE place of the baobab trees, Ma-buyu, was unique
for several reasons. Nowhere else but in the northern part
of the Great Valley existed such a forest of these huge,
grotesque trees, although there is another many hundreds of
miles south-east, in the valley of the Sabi river. But most
astonishing of all, no man, black or white, in all his wanderings,
his explorations and exploitations across the vast valley
territory, has ever become aware of the forest's existence.

The baobab tree is rich in stories of African myth and
magic. No wonder, for it is among the longest-living trees
known, its life measured in thousands rather than in hundreds
of years. The enormous girth, the odd-shaped branches,
twisting eerily upwards, suggest they are capable of movement as, indeed, they are when the Bimbe winds of August

blow strongly from the south-west, across the desert plains and swamps of Namibia and Botswana.

But there was no wind to stir the branches of the baobabs of Ma-buyu on the night Kali-Anuka and Tantalika reached there.

All through the day following their encounter with Kwizima, they plodded on through dense thorn-bush hour after hour, the heavy, humid air pressing down cruelly on them. Kali-Anuka's long, delicate limbs were torn and bleeding, aching all the way down to the tips of his hooves. All day they had met no other animals, and had neither seen nor heard any birds in the stunted trees scattered among the low thorns of the territory they traversed. Then, as evening twilight came, the bushland gave way to a narrow, rock-smooth plateau. To Kali-Anuka, the relief of not having to scour through the thorns was intense; he had rested many times that day, and did so again, lying on the hard, bare surface, his aching, burning body grateful for the touch of the cool rock.

Tantalika looked back at his companion, then ran off across the plateau where it ended abruptly, like the edge of the world. Belly pressed against the surface, he peered over into the void below.

It was as he had seen it, in his mind's eye, this place of Ma-buyu. The great forest of trees far below, the thick, domed trunks reflecting silvery-pink from the imperfect round of the moon, now high above. The forest was enclosed on all sides by vertical cliffs twelve times the height of the trees themselves. All were fully grown, and at this time of the year the branches were thinly decorated with the large, whitish flowers which carry the unpleasant scent of rotting flesh.

He shuffled on all fours along the edge of the cliff, until he found the path he knew to be there, cut with unknown tools by unknown workers, aeons before. It was wide enough for an elephant or a rhinoceros to descend safely, and led straight down to the bottom of the abyss. Calling softly to Kali-Anuka to follow, he had no difficulty in half-running, half-sliding, down to where no sound disturbed the absolute silence, no breath of wind whispered in his ears; and the baobab trees — many hundreds of them — stood deep-rooted in utter immobility.

A long way behind and above him, Kali-Anuka slipped and stumbled down the steep path, bracing his tired legs against the slope. He was not frightened; only bewildered at being so close to the unknown. Then, at last, he was down, standing beside the impatient Tantalika, with the clatter of dislodged stones falling after him, echoing through the silence.

Together they set off for the middle of the forest, where Tantalika had been told to go. Before they reached it they had to skirt round each tree individually, they grew so near to one another.

It was the only clearing in the forest, closely walled by the smooth, round tree-trunks, and they waited there as a cloud passed across the face of the moon, plunging them into darkness. They both lay on the moist sand, Kali-Anuka licking his raw wounds, the otter nibbling at his paws, longing for a mouthful of crab, or fish, he was so hungry.

Suddenly, the moonlight began to flash about the chamber, and the squeaky, yet overwhelming voice of Fura-Uswa came, filling the whole place with its sound.

"Once more I welcome you, otter, but in greater sorrow than the last time. But first I ask you, who is your friend? Can it be Mwami, of the Pambuka, of whom you have spoken so often and praised so highly?"

"No, it is not Mwami," answered Tantalika. "He is dead, and this is his son, Kali-Anuka, who now leads the herd."

"Ah!" Fura-Uswa's exclamation cut the air. "I am pleased, for he must be brave, this impala, as brave as his father, to come with you here.

"Now, otter, I have bad news for you," he went on. "Men have mastered Nyaminyami and me . . . there is no more we can do. They are blind with their own power, and because they want to take the Great Valley for themselves, they have conquered us. We have lost to the madness and greed of these creatures who, I may remind you, were the last animals to be created."

Kali-Anuka raised his head, and with all the vocal strength he could muster, he directed a question at the unseen Fura-Uswa, the question he had asked Tantalika once before.

"But *why* do the Zimikile wish to take the Great Valley from us? *Why* is our valley to drown — what is the purpose?"

"I can tell you why, now I know," the godkin retorted angrily. "It is because they will use the captured waters — by what means even I cannot understand — to give light where there is darkness, to give heat where there is cold, cold where there is warmth, and to make the strength they do not have themselves to drive strange machines which are beyond my comprehension. Man turns everything on earth to his own ends. He believes he is all-powerful, and to him no other creatures are of consequence. But one day, whether in twelve or twelve hundred moons, he will discover there is nothing left, not even himself."

The godkin's voice had dropped to a whispering chitter, yet a deep bitterness was there. When he spoke again, his voice was so quiet that his listeners found it difficult to hear the words.

"After I came here from the Big Rock at the time of Ikando, the spirit go-between of all the birds, Inkwazi the eagle, flew to me and told of more building of this dam, as you call it. The river waters were still flowing there but soon, Inkwazi said, the Zimikile will halt the flow, and we all know what will happen. The highest hills will become islands. The river will no longer be a river, but a lake as wide as the sky . . . and our valley will have gone from sight, for ever."

The voice of the godkin became smaller and smaller; neither Kali-Anuka nor Tantalika could hear it without straining their ears until they ached. There was a distant rumble of thunder, and the fresh smell of rain came on a flutter of wind; once more the moon was obscured by cloud, and the heavy darkness descended over the place of Mabuyu.

"Go now, Tantalika," said Fura-Uswa, calling him by name for the first time. "Go now, Kali-Anuka, and as quickly as possible lead your herd to the safety of the highest hills you can find. Tell others of your kind the same. And you, otter, travel as quickly as your name, carrying my warning to all impala herds, far and wide. I too, have much to do, for although other go-betweens already know what has to be done, many more are coming to me — the elephant-shrew of the elephants, the night-ape of the leopards, the eagle of the big birds, and all the rest . . . so go now, and go well . . . ko caala . . . " and the words of farewell trailed away, receding upwards above the tops of the baobabs, and were lost in the lonely vastness of infinite space.

With the next rumble of thunder, closer now, Tantalika scrambled away, feeling his path through the trees. Kali-Anuka followed close behind, blindly, until a renewed burst of moonlight showed them the steep path which led them, thankfully, to the summit of the cliff.

They crossed the bare rock plateau and sheltered among the thorn-bushes, and for once Tantalika was happy to rest with Kali-Anuka; they were both very tired after their strenuous efforts, and the excitement of the night. The moon shone palely through misty clouds, and the rain, for the time being, held off.

Although without food or comfort, Kali-Anuka's mind was filled with puzzling questions. But, above all, he dearly wanted the answer to one of them.

"How was it," he asked sleepily, "that although Fura-Uswa did not speak in either otter or impala language, we both understood every word he said?"

If Tantalika answered, Kali-Anuka did not hear. His eyes closed, his head drooped, pillowed on the otter's back, and he fell asleep.

There was nothing exceptional about the storm that night; it was one of those which mutter, and pour down token showers of rain as a warning of better things to come. But on the next day the Zambezi river rose to the highest level normally reached at the end of the rainy season, in March or April.

The Pambuka herd, as is customary with most impalas at the start of a new day, was lying down, sleeping or ruminating, and after the period of grooming came the first feeding session, with unweaned lambs suckling their mothers, pausing now and then to rest or play. Little Mupati, at three days old, stayed close to his mother, and always in affectionate sight of Swilila and Silulimi.

Everything seemed perfectly normal. Later, Yandika signalled silently to those who wished to go down to the territorial beach. It was not far away, across a belt of low undergrowth, and down the gentle slope through the trees. But as Yandika led a loosely grouped contingent of impalas down the well-trodden trail, he scented water sooner than usual. There, above the line of the trees, the river seeped between the trunks and the bushes, forming little rivulets which twisted and turned as they probed across the uneven ground, ever-widening. They filled the hollows, and then linked together into larger pools, which in turn spread into miniature lakes, becoming part of the river surface itself. The trees, which before had stood as a screen above the beach, now grew out of the river; the beach, and the grass they loved so much, had disappeared. The river's normally ruffled surface had calmed to a slowly heaving swell.

At first, the significance of all this change did not strike Yandika or the others. It had happened often before — every season, in fact — though never so early, and never in quite the same way, or as quickly. With a gesture equivalent to a shrug of the shoulders, Yandika moved forward to the water and began to drink although he was not thirsty.

But something was wrong, was not as it should be, and Yandika lifted his head more frequently than usual, turning it sharply to right and left, unaware of the danger he sought. His companions became increasingly nervous, some backing away from the creeping waters, frightened to drink.

A sudden wind blew up, and as suddenly died; but it whipped the river into small waves which drove the water even further over the land, and at a snort from Yandika all the impalas wheeled round to flee in close formation to the higher ground they had just left. Together, Swilila and Silulimi joined Yandika, and there was a deep fear in Swilila's eyes.

It was Silulimi who spoke, in an agitated whisper.

"Swilila has just told me of Tantalika's story, on the night before poor Mwami's death," she said. "Do you remember?"

Yandika remembered.

"He warned that if the moon of Nalupale could not be seen, the river would rise, and the Great Valley would drown." She held her words for a moment, and then said: "There was no moon that night, Yandika. That is why Kali-Anuka has gone with the otter to ask Fura-Uswa if this is indeed so. Is that right?"

"I don't know," he said. "I didn't think this was the reason Kali-Anuka went with Tantalika. He told me only that he wanted to prove to himself that the otter spoke the truth. And now" — he turned his head towards the swollen river — "it seems he did."

In the pause that followed, there was a sudden scurrying nearby as a large colony of dassies, flushed out of its warren under a heap of boulders, sped in retreat from the advancing water, barking and whistling in alarm.

"We should go, too," said Silulimi. "We should leave our home range, and go far away up into the hills."

It was not in Yandika's nature to take offence at another's suggestion, even coming from a female, but he was unsure of himself. He hesitated, his front hoof stamping the ground; then, with a toss of his head, he made up his mind.

"We'll stay here for one more night, until Kali-Anuka returns. We'll go into the hills, to our usual place away from the flood, but no further yet. The river, surely, cannot reach there before morning, and then Kali-Anuka, when he comes, will know where to find us, and tell us where to go."

Swilila exchanged a nervous glance with her friend. She looked back as Yandika had done a moment before, towards the river.

"I wonder," she said, very quietly, "if Kali-Anuka will be able to swim the river by then."

High above the gorge at Kariba, early in the morning of the same day, a solitary fish-eagle flew in wide circles, his white neck and head bright in the rays of the hour-old sun. As he glided, using his wings only to turn and keep his height, he did not voice his ringing cry, for he was not on the hunt for fish in the narrow river which tumbled over its rocky bed between the hills below him.

Inkwazi the eagle was a long way from home, a large nest of sticks high in a tall tree upstream where the river was wide and well-stocked with fish. He often flew far afield, but seldom as far as this; the last time was when he had carried the message to Fura-Uswa that the man-made mountain across the gorge had risen again. He did not, of course, fully understand what he saw now, but he knew enough of the ways of men — those wingless birds, as the creatures of the air regarded them — from his countless observations of them from above, to know what they were doing, even if he did not know why they did it.

The massive structure spanning the gorge gleamed white. The great towers of concrete, higher than any tree, joined in a continuous curve, and looked for all the world like the uneven, lower teeth of a giant baboon. At the base of one of these towers, just above the river bed, the waters of the Zambezi were being constricted through a narrow, gridded gap. On a causeway above stood a man wearing a white helmet, and nearby on the river bank were many men who seemed to be watching him, as though his actions were important. Behind him was a long line of huge carriers, filled with boulders.

Inkwazi the eagle swooped low over the scene, so low that his keen eyes could pick out the smallest details. One of them was a round object strapped to the man's left wrist, and had he known of such things, he would have recognised it as a watch. The man kept glancing at it, and eventually raised his right hand, slowly, above his head. Suddenly, he dropped his arm to his side, and the first carrier moved past him and tipped its cargo into the strangled river. The heavy stones hurtled down with a roar, hitting the water in a single splash; for a moment it bubbled and boiled, swirled uncertainly, and then a muddy stain floated to the surface. Another carrier emptied itself; then another.

As Inkwazi flew upwards he saw, below the dam, the river flow checked to a mere trickle; but above the dam there was no flow at all . . . except backwards, upstream.

As he watched, he understood without doubt what these 'wingless birds' had done. He had seen enough and, soaring high in a wide curve, he flew off, westwards, and at last voiced his rasping call. To some of the men below who heard him, familiar with the fish-eagle's call, it sounded different from all others they had heard. It was not a challenging cry, but a cry of despair.

On the first day the waters of the slowly broadening river probed hesitantly to either side; they crept and coiled around rocks and the boles of trees, poured in wide cascades into depressions, and inched higher and higher up the slopes. Gradually, everything that grew close to the ground was obliterated.

The smaller animals, mostly those who dwelt underground, deserted their old haunts; tree dwellers remained, safe for the time being. Larger creatures waited, and moved back only when they had to, trying as best they could to live normally through the day; but uneasily, looking over their shoulders, as it were, at the advancing tide.

Flotsam floated on the thick, muddy water. Dead tree-trunks and branches, sticks and leaves, clung together to form loosely drifting islands. Living, shallow-rooted plants floated to the surface when the soil binding them washed away, and millions of drowned or drowning insects, with no chance of survival, all compacted into solid layers of rubbish, moved flatly inland from the old course of the river.

By sunrise on the second day, the Zambezi had risen twenty feet over its length of 150 miles through the valley, from the age-old gorges at Victoria Falls to the new, man-made barrier at Kariba. Already the face of the valley had changed irrevocably; but it would change again and again, many times, before becoming fully shaped in new perma-nence. All through that day the waters, layered with debris, spread across the riverine forests into the bush beyond, over the plains encircling the hills. Small animals — rats, mice, shrews, hares, and even squirrels — easy prey for eagles and hawks, were helplessly marooned on the islands of matted brushwood which sometimes floated away from the im-permanent shores into the mainstream, blown by the wind.

Up and down the river, for the whole length of the vanishing valley, it was the same. But where the shorelines were rank with vegetation, and the ground was broken or hilly, the tide moved in slowly; where the broad aprons of flat land edged the shores, it swept across rapidly with few obstacles in its way, merging with the simultaneous flooding of the tributaries on either side.

There were many, many tragedies that day in the Great Valley, with thousands more to follow as the days became weeks, the weeks became months, and the months lengthened into years. Yet there was a strange and terrible beauty about the spectacle of a valley which had lived, vibrantly, for millions of years, slowly drowning by the hand of man, to serve him in its death.

7

AS Tantalika and Kali-Anuka journeyed south from the place of Ma-buyu, following the same trail they had covered before, they did not hurry. It was not for lack of urgency to rejoin the Pambuka that Kali-Anuka slackened the pace. He knew only too well that the sooner he got back, the sooner he could carry out a plan to move the herd to safety when the river began to rise. He did not, of course, know when this would be, but it would be best to go, anyway, and find a piece of territory to claim as their own. But hurrying would not help to conserve the strength he would need for swimming the river. His taxing efforts during the past two days had sapped his energy enough already; there had been few opportunities for him to consume sufficient food, and pain shot through his legs and body with every step he took. He could no longer hold up his head, and it drooped down almost between his legs.

In contrast, Tantalika, though covered in festering sores from countless tearing, stabbing thorns, ran buoyantly ahead, taking advantage of every puddle or pool to indulge in a cooling splash and, if he was lucky, a hunting game with a fish, usually ending in a tasty meal. The system worked very well, if unintentionally, for these diversions enabled the stumbling impala to catch up, with the knowledge that there would be water to drink where he found the otter, and then he would enjoy grazing or browsing while Tantalika amused himself.

They had no memorable encounters with other animals, and there were no impalas in this rough country to be told about Fura-Uswa's grim warning. Even though Tantalika scouted round as they approached their resting place of two nights before, he could find no trace of Kwizima or any members of his herd.

So, at the end of the first day on the return journey, they reached the waterfall which trickled down over the ledge into the pool. They did not expect to find many animals there, for the sun had long set, and only the deeply-filtered light from a pale moon, low in the overcast sky, outlined the features of the place. There was a pair of grysbok drinking at the stream, with a single lamb which suckled its mother as she drank; and where the pool narrowed, a solitary male bushpig wallowed, stirring the water to a sandy soup. The bushpig was not alone for long; a sudden crashing of undergrowth a short distance away heralded the arrival of the rest of his party, disdaining the silent caution of most animals when approaching a drinking point. It was as though they were satisfied that  none of their natural enemies were on the prowl.

Kali-Anuka noted this with relief. He was in no shape to

deal with a situation requiring swift retreat. After a brief drink, he browsed for a while off the low bushes near the pool, then retired to ruminate, resting his tired body in long grass near a waterberry tree by the edge of the stream.

The need for sleep overwhelmed Tantalika at last and, after he had satisfied his hunger with a few mouthfuls of fingerlings, he spread his wet body over a slab of rock close to Kali-Anuka, where the pool ran into the stream, and slept.

An otter will sleep for long periods, but an impala — even one as exhausted as Kali-Anuka — never remains asleep for more than a few moments, with all senses remaining wakeful. So Kali-Anuka was first to hear movement from the thick wild gentian bushes downstream. The sound, whatever it was, continued, and soon he saw a small, dark shape moving stealthily, sliding easily over the rocks in the stream, but because of his tiredness, Kali-Anuka was slow to react. Then, suddenly alarmed, he struggled to stand, tensed himself to leap away, when a veering breath of wind carried to his nostrils the scent of otter. Looking down, he saw the flash of white fur between her eyes.

"Vutuka!" he called softly. "Vutuka — I am Kali-Anuka, of the Pambuka!"

The little she-otter paused, standing on her hindquarters just below where he stood, her head to one side, looking up at him from her brown eyes, her long whiskers trembling suspiciously.

He peered down at her over the top of the grass, smiling with his eys, remembering she would not understand his words.

"Kali-Anuka," he repeated, slowly. "Friend of Tantalika," and as he said the name he looked deliberately across to where the otter lay, still asleep.

Vutuka's eyes shone, yellow in a moonbeam as she turned her head to follow his gaze. She reached Tantalika in two or three easy sprints, nipped at one of his ears so that he awoke with a jump; then both otters rolled together into the deep pool, disappearing below the surface to play their underwater game for as long as they could hold in their breath. When at last they came up, Vutuka first, they swam to the far bank, both running over the sand and up the steep slope to the top of the ridge, and away into the night.

Kali-Anuka listened to their ecstatic squeaks and whistles until they became so faint he could hear them no more, and he wondered if they would return that night. He feared not, knowing Tantalika so well; with such a pleasant diversion as Vutuka's arrival, all sense of purpose, all other thoughts would vanish from his mind. Irresponsible — that was the description poor old Mwami had often used when talking about Tantalika. He had been right.

As he stood chewing the remains of a mouthful of cud, Kali-Anuka searched through the dim light, and brought his ears forward to catch any obtrusive sound above that of the water. The little grysbok and the bushpigs had long since departed, but his nostrils worked hard to detect the scent of less welcome visitors. There was nothing; no sounds except from the waterfall, the "hu-hoo-oo" of a pair of owls which came from different directions as they flew from tree to tree, the incessant, raucous toad-calls, and the vibrating song of cicadas. He plucked more leaves, and lay down once more to await, without much hope, Tantalika's return.

He dared not sleep again that night, and when the dim light from the moon vanished as it lowered under the horizon he could see only the white water falling over the ledge and tumbling along over the stones, it was so dark. Unceasingly his ears flicked forwards and sideways, straining for every sound; his nostrils twitched, testing the air for every new scent.

At the first grey glimmer of dawn, he moved quietly away from the pool and into the morning mist which lay thick under the trees. Rather than remain longer, it was better to take a chance in the bush, relying on his emaciated condition to discourage some predator from giving him a second glance. He felt greatly refreshed after the inactivity of the night. He had fed well, and although the sores on his legs still pained him, his muscles ached less, and there was a spring in his step as he found the trail he and Tantalika had followed on their outward journey.

It was a long trek to the river and, if he was to conserve sufficient strength to cross it, he would have to rest frequently on the way. He thought he could reach it before dusk, intending to rest another night before venturing into the water. This would certainly be the most difficult part, for without Tantalika to draw off threatening crocodiles he would be more vulnerable to attack. At the thought, his courage faltered. He stood still for a moment; then braced himself with a reassuring snort and a shake of his head, and resumed walking.

The trail followed downwards to the river, in and out of the valleys between the hills, with the morning sun shafting obliquely through the tree cover and ground mist, forming restless patterns of light and shade. Small creatures scuttered away at his approach, but he met no other, larger ones, and did not look upwards to the woodland birds who screeched and chirped and sang to one another, revelling in the gift of another day.

Four times during the morning he lay down, and then he was clear of the wooded hills, in open ground and looking down on the wide, flat plain stretching before him to the river. It was a relief to see it, and to smell the scent of the river; he only had to negotiate one last, steep descent, before he was on almost level ground. The going would be easier then, despite the many streams to cross, and there was shelter to be had, here and there, where he could rest under the sparsely scattered trees.

But something had changed and at first he was puzzled. It was not because, somewhere on the trail, he had inadvertently strayed from the route he and Tantalika had followed before, and was looking down on the plain from a point further west. Nor was it because the plain was studded, now, with several small herds of animals, some stationary, some moving slowly in one direction or another; always, he noticed, away from the river. Over to his right were zebras and a herd of impala, with many warthogs mingled among them. To his left, kudus, eland and waterbuck circled aimlessly round a low kopje which thrust up, incongruously, above the level plateau. In front of him more impalas, with sable, roan and buffalo for company, grazed placidly on the bright green pasture, and a group of elephants lumbered past them. He could not recollect having seen so many different animals assembled in one place before. But he had seen so little of the world, of the Great Valley, outside his own territory until a few days ago that his knowledge of it was limited.

Straining his eyes, he stretched his gaze beyond the plain to the narrow fringe of trees which marked the river shore, and despite his animal disadvantage of poor vision over great distances he could see what, indeed, had really changed. A cold fear crept over him and grasped at his heart; a front hoof stamped the ground as he realised what had begun to happen.

From his high vantage-point he could see, indistinctly, the wide river sparkling under the high sun, over the tops of the trees by the shore; but now there was a new shoreline on his side of the trees, and long, liquid tentacles crept out across the plain; some of the streams had burst their banks and joined one another to become one. The Great Valley had already begun to drown; just as Fura-Uswa had predicted.

He judged the river to be almost twice as broad as before, and it was hopeless to think he could swim across. He searched his mind for some solution, but found none. Then he saw, far away downstream where the river took a southward bend, a spur of land which rose a little higher than the plateau; here, temporarily at least, the waters were contained and had not yet spilt over the bank. It was his only chance, but he would have to hurry if he was to reach it before sunset or before it was submerged, too.

Tired as he was, he hesitated no longer. He set off, bearing to his left, finding an easy path down the hillside to the flat ground below. It was soothing to feel the soft, close-cropped turf beneath his hooves, and he moved at a steady, loping trot towards his chosen goal. He could have moved faster, speeding along in leaps and bounds, but would soon have exhausted himself, and attracted the attention of the other animals, perhaps starting a disastrous stampede.

He made good progress, passing close to other creatures, but they did not hinder him. Once, as he ran through, breaking up a group of grazing impalas, he called to an old ram he assumed to be their leader.

"Go!" he cried urgently. "Go away from this place, as far as you can — high into the hills where the flood cannot reach you. This is my message from Fura-Uswa!"

But he did not think the ram heard his words, and he dared not pause to repeat them but went on, loath to interrupt the easy, rhythmic pace he had set himself.

He kept this up for a long time, and looking back as he halted under a flat-topped acacia tree he was pleased to see the distance he had covered. But now he had to rest, for the air was heavy with heat and he must have relief from the burning afternoon sun which seemed to scorch the tender flesh beneath his skin.

He remained in the scanty shade of the tree long enough to chew some of its velvety pods and to nibble at the grass; then he lay for a while, ruminating. Soon he was off again, in a wide sweep round the little kopje he had seen earlier, skirting the upper reaches of a small stream that had swelled to a river, almost cutting him off from his objective. He rested again twice, before he started to climb the gradient which would bring him to the low promontory above the turn of the river.

His pace began to flag, then. Although the slope was smooth, he stumbled a lot because his legs were weakening and he was losing control of them. But he persevered, and when his shadow moving beside him thinned to a drawn-out parody of himself, he felt he had come far enough. Turning towards the river, he raced in one last frantic effort down through thick, tangled jesse to the water's edge, collapsing in a heap among the debris of dead sticks, leaves and branches, at the bottom of a deep donga.

For a long time he lay there, his breath coming in short gasps, his head resting uncomfortably on a pillow of dry sticks, but he could not raise it up. His overworked legs twitched and no longer seemed to be attached to his body. Mind dulled by his exertions, he had no clear thoughts and did not know what he was doing here, or how he had come. His power of thought ebbed away, and he gave himself up to the situation completely; his eyes closed and he lost consciousness.

For the first time ever in early summer, the Pambuka herd had moved up into the low foothills above their home range. But they did not go far enough; Yandika had been mistaken when he had assured the two does that the flood would not reach there by morning. It had, and inundated the area so deeply that the impalas had to move away before the sun had risen, and long before there could be any chance of Kali-Anuka attempting his return crossing.

So the herd trekked a little further, a little higher this time. Yandika could not be persuaded to go far, to leave the territory that had been Pambuka stamping ground for as long as even Mwami could remember, when he still lived. It was wrong, Yandika said firmly, and without Kali-Anuka's agreement, he could not do it.

"We must wait for him, however long it may be."

Silulimi shook her head.

"No, Yandika — we cannot." She glanced quickly round to satisfy herself neither Swilila nor Kusomona were near. "Kali-Anuka will not come back, of that I'm sure," she said quietly, and pretended to nuzzle Yandika's face so that her mouth was close to his ear. "How could he swim the river now? It's twice as wide as before, and no impala that has ever lived could have swum so far."

"Mwami could have!" Yandika snorted. "And so can Kali-Anuka!"

"Don't fool yourself," she retorted, still whispering. "We cannot be sure, even, that Kali-Anuka succeeded in reaching the other side. But if he did, there's no way he can get back now, unless he grows wings."

"We shall see." That was all Yandika said.

Impatiently, Silulimi moved away.

"I respect your loyalty — if that is what it is," she said over her shoulder, "but it may be the death of us all, Yandika."

She left him feeling confused and alone, more than a trifle disappointed with himself. A leader should lead, he asserted, and all he was doing was to put off an important decision, hoping against all odds that Kali-Anuka would soon return to relieve him of the burden of responsibility. If Silulimi was right, and he did not come back, the river might suddenly rise so quickly that escape would be impossible; the Pambuka — all of them — would be no more than food for the crocodiles. He trembled at the thought, lowered his mouth to the grass and began to graze, putting out of his mind such dreadful ideas, and the problems facing him.

Away from their home range, in strange and unfamiliar surroundings, every member of the herd, except the very young, felt uncomfortable with nerves stretched more tautly than ever before. A flurry of dead leaves in a breath of wind sent them scattering as though a leopard or a lion had suddenly leapt among them. Even the friendly tick birds, feasting off their body parasites, annoyed them so much that now and then both rams and does shook them off angrily, the little birds twittering huffily as they flew away; but they came back, persistently.

The impalas were continually disturbed by other animals who trespassed on their temporary territory, fleeing from their own waterlogged haunts; they were not aggressive, but they were unwelcome. Not belligerent by nature, the impalas could do little to drive the intruders away, but untypically some of the younger rams chased or charged at smaller antelopes — grysbok or, frequently, duikers — and docile does, especially with young, harassed them with mock charges, harmless enough but indicative of the high state of tension which had electrified the herd. There was only one casualty, when a yearling ram encountered a lone, scaly pangolin, who rolled himself into a tight ball when the ram shoved him rudely with his blunt horns. The pangolin then lashed out with his tail, scything the impala across his muzzle and tearing the flesh painfully.

The day wore on, and by mid-afternoon the herd had received no signal from Yandika to move further up into the hills. Silulimi spoke to him again, and even Swilila approached him to voice her own soft-spoken opinion. But the leader would not listen, and stood his ground.

"We will go when Kali-Anuka is here to tell us," he said, "or, if it comes sooner, when the water forces us to go."

They were near enough to the river to hear a sound which froze them into alert immobility. It was a familiar sound to all of them, and it spelt danger. It was the noise of a Zimikile carrier-creature, travelling on the water, coming from the west a long way upstream. But because it was a heavier, louder throbbing than any heard before, it suggested a greater threat to them. One of the older rams, remembering the sharp explosion when the lamb fell at its mother's hooves onto the sand, and again when Mwami had died, associated these incidents with the noise he now heard, and his tight nerves snapped. In panic he forgot his lowly status, snorted a warning, and hurtled away into the bush. Nerves broke behind him and, unthinking, the rest of the herd wheeled round in confusion, before bounding away after him in long, springing leaps.

Only Swilila, Silulimi, Kusomona and her lamb remained, with a bewildered Yandika.

"Why did he do that, the old fool?" he protested. "The carrier can't harm us, so far away."

Swilila, trembling with the fear transmitted by those who had fled, came close to Yandika.

"Now we shall have to go," she said, her voice faltering, "or we shall die alone."

He was a big fellow, the python watching the unconscious Kali-Anuka, big enough to swallow a small impala whole. He was coiled high on the forked branches of a dead tree over-hanging the donga, not with any intention of ambushing prey but simply because he was tired after a long swim from his favourite hunting-ground upstream, a reedbed close to the shore, teeming with waterbirds which he often fancied as a change of diet from rodents, hares or small antelope. But with the rising water the birds had flown and, quite at home as a powerful swimmer, he had decided to seek another, similar source of food downriver. Not up-to-date with the news of impending disaster in the valley, nor gifted with great intelligence, it did not occur to him that his search would be fruitless, for nowhere along the river were there reedbeds any more; all had vanished and the waterbirds' nests and un-hatched chicks with them. So, by the time he reached the steep bank at the river bend, he was not only very tired, but very hungry. He swam through the floating crust of debris which nudged against the bank, and then came up where the open end of the donga entered the water. Snaking up over the decaying vegetation piled on its bed, he enjoyed himself for a time seizing several large rats as they burrowed desperately into the mould, seeking escape from his lightning strikes. Then, his immediate hunger satisfied, he curled his great length round the forked branches, and composed himself for sleep.

It was the noise of Kali-Anuka's fall, the snapping of twigs and branches, that awakened him. He was too tired to care very much what had caused the sudden, disturbing sounds; but to ensure there was no danger at hand, he uncoiled the head end of his body and lowered it downwards, hissing menacingly. The small eyes in his spear-shaped head stared at the awkwardly recumbent impala for a long time, weighing up the desirability of foregoing his interrupted sleep to make a meal of it. Easy meat, he thought; there would be a struggle, and he would have preferred a doe — a ram's horns could be troublesome to his digestion. This ram was a bit big anyway. Oh yes, he decided as he stretched for a closer look with his short-sighted eyes — much too big, though there's not much flesh on him.

The branch he lay on cracked suddenly under his unevenly balanced weight. The sharp report echoed across the river, and he fell with a crash into the mess of compost below. Kali-Anuka snapped out of his sleep, scrambled clumsily to his hooves, and blundered through the tangle of brushwood up on to firm ground. He leapt away, far enough from the donga to feel safe from what he thought to be a Zimikile armed with a banging stick. He stood trembling with reaction from the shock he had suffered. He sniffed for man-scent, and listened; but he could hear nothing unusual, and could smell only the python.

When he was calmer, he looked down through the trees at the river. It appeared broader than he had judged earlier. Even had he felt in peak condition he doubted his chances of getting across, crocodiles or no crocodiles.

An afternoon storm was gathering, black and menacing over the hills behind him, and with the sun low in the sky there was no time to lose. He must attempt the impossible now, or there would never be another chance, for overnight the river would widen even more; by morning he would be cut off from his Pambuka for ever, which would be worse than the death he was now facing.

He walked up and down a few times, breaking into short runs, or bucking like a zebra, loosening his stiff, aching limbs. He eased himself down the steep bank and into the heaving layer of rubbish which floated on the water; its cool, wet touch instantly refreshed him. He struck out, swimming easily with only his head and the top of his back above the surface. Beyond a few scattered, partly submerged trees on the oppostite shore was a long, grassy mound, and he aimed for this, encouraged to find the river calm, gently swelling; there was no strong current to sweep him off his course. Less than a third of the way across, he had to admit to himself that it was hopeless. He had tired so quickly that all the strength had gone out of his legs; he could barely hold up his head, under the weight of his horns, to keep his eyes and nose exposed to the air.

It meant nothing to him when he heard a heavy, mechanical throbbing sound which grew louder and louder until it drummed into his head, and he could feel the vibrations feathering against his body under the water. What it was, had he bothered to wonder, was of no consequence now that he was near the point of inevitable death. But a last determined effort to survive was stimulated when he remembered a lesson Mwami had taught him during their early swimming lessons. He tried it, and filled his lungs with air. With the extra

buoyancy, he struck out with his front legs until he was forced to exhale, before taking another great breath. He worked his legs again, briefly; then exhaled, breathed in again to regain buoyancy, and paddled for another short distance. He repeated these actions, over and over, but it was no use; he was too far gone. Each time he let out his breath he sank lower in the water, his mouth filling with it, spluttering, choking, sometimes with only his nose, and the tips of his horns above the surface, inhaling a mixture of air and water.

The drumming sound overwhelmed him now, and seemed to press him down. For what he was sure was the last time, his head bobbed up, his front legs pawed at the water, and in those few seconds he glimpsed a dark, shadowy shape close to him. Something flashed over his head; there was a splash, and then another. A firm support came under his chest, just below his neck, and his horns were gripped so that his head remained above water and he could take gulping breaths again. Too weak to struggle, he resigned himself, for the second time, to meet his end, and he waited for the silence; but it did not come.

On either side of him were pale Zimikile creatures, one with his hand against his chest, the other holding on to his horns. He could feel himself being steered by these men towards the dark shape which throbbed, quietly now, riding the water nearby. They spoke, and voices answered from the floating carrier, all harsh-sounding to Kali-Anuka, so much uglier than the soft voices of animals; and, of course, he did not understand anything they said.

Two black Zimikile reached down and lifted his limp body into the boat, lowering him gently on to the metal floor; he was surprised that he was not flung down carelessly. The men in the water, both stripped to the waist, climbed after him. One knelt beside him while the other opened a box and rummaged inside.

Breathing in short, sharp gasps, Kali-Anuka looked at the man's face bent close over his, and thought he saw kindness and compassion in his eyes. The thin mouth in the rugged features widened, and the eyelids contracted, the skin around them wrinkling in small folds. He felt the touch of the man's rough hand on his cheek, softly caressing, and the voice lost its harshness, becoming low and soothing. He could not believe, even then, that the Zimikile meant no harm; and at the instant the hypodermic needle stabbed into his rump he had no time for his disbelief to be confirmed, for he blacked-out immediately.

The man who had administered the mild tranquillising drug grinned at his companion, and they talked together for a while as the boat slowly gathered speed from its aging motor, heading for the shore, to the very place Kali-Anuka had been aiming to reach. It steered in among the half-drowned trees, blunt bow thrusting aside the floating debris in shallow water and, the engine cutting back, gently drifted broadside to where the grass of the mound grew below the water which lapped the new-formed shoreline. One of the black men stood up and grasped an overhanging branch, steadying the boat, and for a while it remained lightly rocking in the calm water as the men talked among themselves. They discussed the lateness of the afternoon, pointing at the sun as it turned to deep orange over the western hills, and then at the darkly bruised sky to the north. It was a long way downriver to the base camp, and they must reach there before the hazards of a stormy night overtook them. They kept glancing at Kali-Anuka, lying motionless in the well of the boat, breathing more easily and regularly as the effects of the drug began to work. He should come out of it soon, they said, enough to put him ashore. And let it be quickly, one added, because now the mosquitoes were coming at them in great whirling clouds, their high-pitched humming surrounding the men whose flesh was already punctured and swollen.

Kali-Anuka moved his head slightly, and his glazed eyes opened. His legs kicked out as he tried to raise himself to his hooves, but he bungled the attempt as the men came to him, tipping the boat over to one side. The tall man who had smiled at him dropped into the knee-deep water as the two others gripped the impala's legs, lifting him carefully over the side of the boat. There was a feeble struggle, but Kali-Anuka was still befuddled with the drug, and his resistance was instinctive and quite ineffectual. The man in the water turned the animal to face dry land, and with a light, affectionate slap on the rump and an encouraging shout, set Kali-Anuka on his way to safety, at last, splashing through the water and staggering up on to the grass.

He looked back and met, fleetingly, the man's eyes, dark

under the brim of a tall bush hat, before he turned away. The
men climbed back in the boat, and with a burst of power it
swung round and headed out into midstream, zigzagging
between the waterlogged trees, to continue its journey to the
base camp, several miles downriver towards the dam.

8

DARKNESS came quickly that evening. As the sun fell from sight, the great blanket of storm-clouds, heavy with rain and streaked with unceasing, hissing shafts of lightning, engulfed the sky to the limits of the horizon. The ground trembled under the angry peals of thunder, and the tall mahogany trees, not so high now above the flood, flung their heavily-branched heads about in the tearing wind, wrenching at their age-old roots which clung fast to the subsoil, softening quickly as the water seeped far down below.

The valley — the land and the hills, the trees and the river, the heavy clouds above — wept in a great flood of tears as it began to die its slow and lingering death. No living thing escaped the saturation coming from every side, except the few who had heard of Fura-Uswa's warning, had acted upon it and had fled to high ground. Despite the humid heat of the stormy night, all shivered with a terrible, cold fear that life, whether the gift of a day or a century, would soon come to an end. As though they were obedient to some mute command, but in reality bewildered beyond understanding, there was no hunting or killing that night. The night-birds huddled deep in their nests in the swaying trees; brave or cunning hunting creatures cowered in the penetrating dampness of their lairs; prey usually anticipating attack stood miserably alert, waiting only for this overwhelming wetness to cease when, with the warmth of a sunrise, if it ever came, all would be dry again.

For half the night the storm rampaged over the whole length and breadth of the valley, and beyond. Then, as its intensity waned, the tempestuous wind blew itself into quiescence, and the streaking rain thinned to a dismal drizzle. All was quiet, and the silence was immense.

Under a wild fig-tree, growing out of a cluster of small rocks in open ground, four impalas stood, their hooves sunk deep in the mud which oozed about them. They were close together, touching, and each could feel the other's body shivering against his own, in fear and dampness. Another, Kusomona's lamb Mupati, stood under his mother's belly, less frightened now that the storm had spent itself but not liking what he had, so far, seen and heard of life in the world. There was only one thing that had given him pleasure and, as if reminded of it, he reached up to suck at his mother's generous udders again. Kusomona, at the touch of his hungry mouth, shifted her position and her hooves squelched in the mud. Her companions lifted their hooves, too, and were stimulated into a discussion of their plight.

"How much longer must we stay here?" Silulimi asked, directing her question at Yandika, shivering beside her.

He did not answer immediately, but gazed fixedly into the gloom of the rain-washed night, seeing nothing except the curtain of fine rain falling close to his eyes. He was certain that he had been mistaken in his earlier decision, to stay so close to the river. But he would not admit it, except to himself.

"We will go when it's light," he said flatly. "The others won't have gone far — we should find them soon."

"If we do," said Silulimi dubiously, "you won't be welcome, Yandika. You'll have to fight for your leadership."

"Perhaps I will. But remember, Kali-Anuka is still our leader."

"Kali-Anuka is dead," Swilila said with certainty in her voice, though it trembled a little. "We will never see him again."

A long silence followed this dismal pronouncement, but they could hear Mupati pulling noisily at his mother's teats. The thin drizzle eased, but large drops of moisture dripped from the fig-tree, showering heavily as the laden branches stirred with each gust of trailing wind.

As though a dim light had been turned on over the eastern hills, the dark sky brightened. Stars appeared momentarily in breaks in the clouds, only to flicker and vanish into the yellowing dawn sky. The sun heaved upwards, gilded and fresh, seeming to push the sharply defined edge of cloud canopy across the sky and over the far horizon, dispelling something of the profound sense of doom which had fallen over the valley during the night.

But it cannot be said that life returned to normal for all creatures, trees and growing things of the Great Valley. Many had died, or were dying, and it was far removed from normal for crocodiles to find whole carcases floating about the flooded river, to be picked up for the taking. It was anything but normal for brushwood islands to drift about, carrying baboons and snakes, monkeys and bushbabies, all puzzled at such strange events, and too terrified to pick deadly quarrels among themselves, which would have been expected of them had they followed natural instinct. Nor was it normal that many animals could not find the food of their usual diet and, in time, would die of starvation.

The place where Yandika and the others had sought refuge for the night was a smooth, almost treeless slope, small in area, on fairly high ground. A few sapling figs grew weakly near the parent tree sheltering them, but there was little other vegetation growing in the impoverished soil. What there was had mostly been cropped already by other animals. The stony ground was scarred with shallow dongas, all deepening towards the lowest edge of the slope, nearest to the river. Except for lizards and insects and a few green pigeons in the fig-tree, no other life was about. Over the topmost edge the ground fell away, gradually, in natural terraces, strewn with boulders and a few stunted bushes, whose roots clung tenuously to pockets of soil between the rocks.

It was far from an ideal habitat in which impalas could remain for long, and the four adults yearned for the luxurious offerings of their own home territory.

"Let's feed here on what we can, and then we'll move on," Yandika said.

Moving out from the long shadow of the tree into the brightening sunshine of the new day, they browsed on the young fig-leaves which were within reach. Silulimi expressed her disgust at the unpleasant taste, turning to nibble at a minute patch of grass nearby.

"Even the grass tastes foul," she said, tearing it out by the roots.

They fed for a long time, and their coats, soaked from the rain, soon dried under the mounting warmth of the sun. Although there was plenty of water in pools and puddles along the dongas, they did not need to drink, taking enough moisture with the leaves to satisfy their thirst.

Yandika turned to the others as they began to ruminate.

"Stay here," he said, "while I scout around and find the best way to go."

He did not bother to go back the way they had come, for he knew that by now the flood was there to block their escape. He walked up to the highest edge, where he could look down and assess what route they could take, to bring them to even higher ground and acceptable pasture.

It was hot now, with steam rising from the wet earth under his hooves, and already the mud was crusting as he climbed. He looked back several times at the others, still in the open, close to the fig-trees. They seemed safe enough, and he felt grateful for the absence of other animals. A short distance from his starting point he reached the highest limit of the hills, and hidden among low bushes he peered down at the vista lying before him.

Below the terraces, where the day before there had been a broad, heavily wooded valley, there was now an expanse of water, patterned with the crowns of trees, and everything was so still it could always have been like that. Here and there between the trees, patches of clear water rippled, stroked by touches of the wind, glinting silver under the sun.

Yandika looked over to his left, and there was water. He looked to his right — and there was water. He guessed correctly that he and his female charges now occupied an island, and unless they attempted to swim away from it they could not escape. He knew, without doubt, they could not survive for long; it would be just a few days at most before they would consume the little available pasture which grew around them. Perhaps, before then, the ground they stood on would be swamped, too; they would swim a little and, soon exhausted, quickly drown.

He tossed his head, trying to free his mind from such thoughts but could not. His front hoof stamped down, but the more he stamped the more perplexed he became. He braced himself to tell the others of the fate that awaited them, turned from the vantage-point, and walked slowly and dejectedly down towards the fig-trees.

"Look at him," said Silulimi contemptuously. "His nose almost touches the ground as he walks. It must be bad news he's bringing."

Kusomona, who never spoke much, rose to her hooves as Yandika approached.

"He's worried, Silulimi. You can see that."

"Don't be too hard on him," added Swilila. "He's done his best, after all."

"But his best isn't good enough for us," Silulimi snapped back, and as the ram rejoined the group, raising his head to confront them with his news, she said: "What now, O Leader?"

The deliberate mockery was lost on him.

"We're trapped," he said positively. "There's water all around us, as broad as the river, and we must stay here until we die."

Silulimi's soft eyes hardened as she looked full at him.

"That's the quickest decision you've made so far," she said bitterly. "You're our leader, Yandika, and you must think of something better than that!"

He looked back at her.

"Can you swim, Silulimi?" he asked. "Can any of us swim more than a few impala lengths? Can Mwami-Mupati?"

The others were hushed by his questions. They all knew the answers, and even Silulimi found nothing to say.

Swilila sighed, and it was echoed by Kusomona.

"If only Kali-Anuka were here," said the one.

"*He* can swim," said the other proudly.

"But he's not here," Silulimi said testily, "and even if he were, the fact that he can swim wouldn't be much help to us, not if there's as much water as you say."

Suddenly Yandika raised his head, and his nostrils quivered. The others straightened up, sniffing the air. Four impala necks stretched up to their limits, and four pairs of nostrils all pointed in the same direction, down towards where the river had flowed.

Yandika was the first to identify the scent, and he took a deep breath to shout louder than he had ever done before, startling himself with the power of his voice.

"Tantalika!" he called.

"Tantalika!" called the others, joyously.

This was too much for little Mupati, who ran under his mother's belly in fright.

They called again and again. The name tumbled like a birdcall through the air, hovering long enough above the tops of the drowning trees at the foot of the slope for the otter to hear it.

Swimming slowly through the tangle of sodden vegetation, brushing floating sticks and branches aside with his whiskered muzzle, Tantalika cleared a watery path for his mate Vutuka, who paddled close behind him. He headed towards the undefined shoreline, where the water lapped the flat mound where the impalas were prisoners. Busy with his navigational difficulties he could not call back, but his senses told him exactly where they were. Soon both otters splashed out of the water and in a few moments were hurrying over the ground on their short legs, backs arched and tails up-tilted. The impalas' eyes shone a welcome, and Tantalika, in his joy at finding them, ran round in circles, in and out between their legs, playing the game he had often played before. Then he saw Mupati backing against his mother's forelegs, apprehensive of this strange creature he had never seen before. The otter stood before him, and looked him up and down appraisingly.

"This must be Kali-Anuka's son," he said. "Am I right?" He glanced up at Kusomona for confirmation.

"Yes," she said, "and he is called Mwami-Mupati. But — but where is Kali-Anuka? Why is he not with you?"

Tantalika showed surprise. He turned his head, but the only ram he saw was Yandika.

"He's not here ? Then I don't know where he is."

All the impalas spoke at once, asking questions, angrily accusing: why did you separate, where did you leave him? You should have stayed together, you're irresponsible — just as Mwami always said. Why did you let him go with you in the first place? Oh, Tantalika — how could you lose him?

The otter listened to them in silence, and when they had

finished he sat up in his three-pointed way, put the fingers of his paws together, and as Vutuka nestled against him as though giving him support, he spoke.

He told them in his fast little voice how Vutuka had bitten his ear as he slept by the waterfall, and how, in their joy of reunion, they had run off together and played, savouring their togetherness after so many days of separation.

"We didn't leave Kali-Anuka for long," he said, "only until morning, but when we came back he had gone — and he must have left very early because we found it difficult to find his spoor under the dew. Then we lost it where a herd of zebra had trampled about, and although we tried very hard we couldn't pick it up again. I thought he would have followed the same trail we had come by, but he must have strayed off somewhere, enough for us to lose him. I still didn't worry — Kali-Anuka, as we all know, is no fool — and I felt sure he would have no problem finding his way back to you."

"Was he well when you last saw him?" asked Kusomona.

Tantalika hesitated.

"As well as could be expected after his experiences, I would say," he answered, guardedly.

He did not want to tell Kusomona, or any of them, of Kali-Anuka's true condition — weakened and wasted to a shadow of his former self, near complete physical collapse, and that it was only his remarkable courage and determination that had kept him going. He knew nothing of the rest of his journey, of course, and secretly held out little hope that he could have completed it. But he mentioned nothing of these things.

"I think the time has come when those of us who do not know should be told what is happening, and how it has all come about," said Silulimi, firmly. "Kali-Anuka confided in Yandika and Swilila before he went away, I understand, and it was quite correct for him to do so. But now there are few of us, with only Kusomona and I the ignorant ones. We're all in the same predicament and we, too, have a right to know everything. What is this flooding all about, so early in the season? Why did Kali-Anuka go away with you, Tantalika, and where did you go? We know some of the answers, but we should know all of them."

"You should indeed know of these things, Silulimi," agreed Tantalika. "All animals, all birds, should know of them but everything has happened so quickly that it has not been possible. I was charged to inform every leader of every impala herd in the Great Valley. But I have failed in my task because there hasn't been time to accomplish it." He drew a deep breath, and shook his head. "Bear with me, Silulimi, Kusomona, and I will tell you as soon as I can. But now is not the time, for there are many things to be done if you are to be saved, and the Pambuka herd made whole again. There is nothing more important than that. Now, Yandika," — he turned to the acting leader — "now, where are all the others?"

Yandika told him how they had all run off on the previous day, at the sound of the floating carrier-creature coming down the river. He told him how he and the three does, with Mupati, had waited for Kali-Anuka before following the others' example, and had spent the last terrible night on this small refuge, now isolated by the floodwaters.

Tantalika listened to his tale patiently. He did not criticise Yandika's wisdom, although he thought it foolish of him, as had Silulimi, not to have moved even further away before being cut off.

"All right," he said. "We must make a plan."

But before he could speak of his proposal, Swilila and Kusomona, almost in unison, interrupted him with the question uppermost in their minds.

"Is Kali-Anuka alive? Will he come back?"

Tantalika dropped on all fours, sniffing at the bare ground as though seeking an answer. Vutuka slipped away to explore under some of the stones nearby, hoping to find some small thing to eat.

"We must hope so," said Tantalika, quietly. "Perhaps he managed to swim the river before it climbed over the banks. Perhaps he is still over on the other side. I do not know, but tomorrow I will search for him."

"Tomorrow?" chorused four impala voices, astonished. "Not until tomorrow?"

"Why not today?" Silulimi stamped a hoof. "By tomorrow we may all be dead! Drowned!"

"There's not enough food for us here," added Yandika.

Tantalika looked up at them quizzically.

"So even if I found Kali-Anuka today," he said, "he couldn't help you in your plight, could he? And if he is alive now, he may join you in death tomorrow, from what you say. Listen," he went on, "I'm going to look around this place, which I know quite well already. Maybe I'll find a way to get you to higher ground; then, tomorrow at sunrise I can go off to search for Kali-Anuka, and if I find him, can bring him to you. Across the river, if necessary," he added with confidence.

So the matter rested. A plan had been made and although Silulimi grumbled she was thankful that there was a decision at last, however slim its chances of success. Swilila and Kusomona, their hopes for Kali-Anuka's survival a little higher now, put their trust in Tantalika, and began grazing on

the scant tufts of grass, while Mupati once more moved in
hungrily to his own source of sustenance.

Yandika, without a word of protest but with secret relief,
had therefore abandoned his authority over the depleted
herd to an otter.

Moving with his accustomed swiftness, it did not take
Tantalika long to reconnoitre the boundary of the island. He
dropped into the water along the irregular shoreline, testing
the depth where no trees or bushes grew to guide him. He
swam out, his belly sometimes brushing the bed, or diving
where it was deep; then he backtracked, seeking a shallower
path which the impalas could tread without having to swim
more than a few, easy lengths.

At last he fixed the route
they could take, but to make
sure it was safe he traversed
it several times, learning it
off by heart until he knew
every obstacle that might
cause trouble. Of his arch-
enemy, the crocodile, there

was no sign. He worried more about the rapidly rising water;
there was no time to lose if the impalas were to wade across
before being engulfed.

On the far side the bank lifted clear, up into a broad hill
which folded back into another, even higher, where he could
see green grass and scattered mopane thickets. For a time, at
least, this would be an ideal habitat for the impalas. And if the
floodwaters lifted quickly, there were more hills rolling back
beyond.

Pleased with his success, certain that when the time
came any difficulties could easily be overcome, he hurried
back to the five impalas. He wasted no time with explanations,
but called to Vutuka, and led the company to the southerly
point of the island he had selected for their entry into the
water.

"We can never swim that distance!" Silulimi exclaimed in horror, when she saw the great expanse of water laid before them.

"Silulimi," said Tantalika patiently, "you won't have to swim. If you all follow me, without wandering either to right or left, even your white bellies won't get wet."

"But . . . Mupati," ventured Kusomona. "What about him?"

"I've thought of that," Tantalika said, "and noticed how strongly he sucks for his milk." His teeth snapped together rapidly as he laughed. "Let him suck at your tail for a change, Kusomona. With Vutuka behind him, to warn us if he falls, he'll be all right."

It was a strange procession that threaded its way through the water. Tantalika led, half-swimming most of the way, lowering himself now and then so that his paws touched the bottom, checking the depth. He was followed by Silulimi, grumbling all the time, treading warily and screaming in panic whenever she slipped into a small depression. Behind her was Swilila, and then Kusomona towing Mupati with her tail; young as he was, he soon entered into the spirit of the game, relinquishing his hold, splashing happily through the water on his own. Vutuka kept her fingered paws ready to steady him had he strayed off the trail of his mother's steps. Last in the line came Yandika, feeling a little foolish that he had not considered the depth of the flooding earlier.

There were no crocodiles, and only small pieces of floating debris to hinder them. The bed they walked on undulated slightly, but they trod on soft, short grass and there were no hidden hazards; Tantalika had seen to that. It was difficult climbing the steep bank on the other side, for it was thickly strewn with loose rocks; twice Swilila and Silulimi, ahead and above Yandika, dislodged small boulders which tumbled down, hitting him glancing blows on his chest and head. But he suffered no injuries.

It was after sundown when they came to the grassed and wooded summit of the hill Tantalika had seen. The impalas revelled in their return to a normal diet, stuffing their mouths with grass. When they were satisfied, they relaxed, and heedless of potential danger they ruminated in deep contentment under the mopanes.

Tantalika, who with Vutuka had gone off on a brief but rewarding hunting trip, returned to tell them his plan of action.

"Much as I would like to," he began, "I'm not going to search for Kali-Anuka tonight. It's too dangerous, for even if none of you have noticed — being so busy filling your bellies — there are many of your enemies about. I can scent leopards and lions on the wind; I can hear wild dogs and hyenas not far away. When Vutuka and I were catching rats, we saw a pair of caracals prowling through the bush. Perhaps, just as we have found refuge from the flood, so have they — they're all about us, and probably hungry. Hungry enough to eat otters, I dare say.

"Your senses may be dulled a little, after all your suffering these past few days. But we must all remain on our guard, more than ever, during the night. I will try for as long as I can to keep you entertained, by telling you all you wish to know," — he looked pointedly at Silulimi — "and then I will tell you of some strange happenings which Vutuka and I saw after we lost Kali-Anuka's trail."

Swilila was reminded of that night, so very long ago, when Tantalika had sat before the group of impalas under the buffalo-thorn tree in their home range, now gone for ever beneath the flood-waters. The moon of Kanini shone down on them then, but now it was the moon of Nalupale, and it shone weakly through thin, scurrying clouds. She thought of the four impalas who had listened to the otter, but only two were here this time — herself and Yandika. Mwami, dear Mwami, had gone — and only Fura-Uswa knew where; Kali-Anuka, her brave and wise son, was gone, too, but although in her mind she was sure he would never return, she heard a whispering voice in her heart telling her he still lived.

She did not listen to Tantalika's story of his journey to the Big Rock, his discussion with Fura-Uswa, or the reasons for it all; she had heard it once before. But when he told of his trek with Kali-Anuka to the place of Ma-buyu, of what had happened there, her ears came forward with renewed interest.

After he and Vutuka had lost Kali-Anuka's trail, they went on to the swollen river and swam between the trees to a little island. From another, larger one came the shouting voices of Zimikile, and three zebras — a male and two females — galloped out of the bushes, snorting and whistling in fear. Then four Zimikile ran out, waving sticks and branches as they shouted at the animals. One of the mares went into the water first.

"I had never seen a zebra swim before, and now I know why," said Tantalika. "She didn't swim very far, only the length of six otters, from nose to tail. Her head sank lower and lower, until only her tail and the top of her backside were above water. She sank, but came up again thrashing about . . . and then she rolled over and died, and her body floated away." He paused, then added: "I think she must have been with foal."

He hastened on with his story. The stallion and the other mare were driven into the water by two Zimikile, who followed them in. A floating carrier, which had been hidden among the trees, nosed out and encircled the swimmers. Tantalika could not explain how it was done but eventually both zebras were lifted, in turn, out of the water and on to the carrier.

"It swam away," he went on, "and passed close by Vutuka and me. We followed it, staying underwater so that the Zimikile wouldn't see us. Soon the carrier slowed, and

swam into the water's edge under a long hill. Two Zimikile
jumped into the shallows, helped those on the carrier to lift
out the zebras, who both ran off up the hill as fast as their legs
could carry them. One of the Zimikile — whose face was quite
dark but not black — took off his head-cover and threw it up
into the air.'' Tantalika stroked his chin, and shook his head.
"I don't know why he did that. But, then," he added, "I
cannot understand any of the things that were done."

There was silence from Tantalika's audience.

"Perhaps," Yandika said at last, "they were just playing
some game."

"Or they wanted to find out if zebras can swim,"
suggested Swilila. "I've often heard that the Zimikile are
always wanting to find out about everything."

"Perhaps they *knew* zebras cannot swim very well, and
were trying to save them from starving on the island, when the
food was all gone," ventured Kusomona, charitably.

"Or from drowning when the water came higher," Swilila
added.

Silulimi snorted with contempt.

"That doesn't sound like the way of Zimikile!" she said.
"I expect Yandika was nearer the mark — it was just a
horrible game, and if they'd had sticks with them, they would
have gone off bang at them in the end."

"But they *had* sticks!" Tantalika said quickly. "They
hung over the shoulders of two of them, when they were on the
island."

There was another long silence after this. But it was
Tantalika who closed the discussion.

"I think Swilila — and Kusomona — may be right," he
said thoughtfully. "There must be *some* good Zimikile in the
world, and I must say that once they started getting hold of
the zebras they were very gentle with them." He sighed. "But
perhaps we will never know for certain."

The little group of impalas had become so engrossed in
the otter's story they had forgotten his earlier warning to keep
all their senses alert for dangerous intruders. But they need
not have worried, for Vutuka, not understanding impala

language, had soon become bored, and occupied herself
moving around among the trees, acting as a self-appointed
guard.

All through the night they were left undisturbed, and
soon after the sun had risen, Tantalika left them to search for
Kali-Anuka.

9

NEVER before in his life had Kali-Anuka wished so much for sleep. After his instinctive burst of running leaps away from the Zimikile and their floating carrier, across the grass and into the sheltering trees further over the mound, he halted, and swayed on his weakening legs. His breath came in long, laboured gasps, his head ached and throbbed as though dung-beetles battered solid balls of dung against his skull. His sight was blurred, and even the trunks of the small trees surrounding him merged into a grey, shapeless mist. When a hamerkop flew down from its massive domed nest in the fork of a tall tree in front of him, snatching a frog from the ground, Kali-Anuka backed away in fright, not recognising the crested bird for what it was.

With the pain racking his body, the agony in his head, he

wanted nothing more than to sleep. He fought against the
fierce urge, his confused mind sufficiently aware that the
water lapping close behind could soon engulf him if he lay
down and surrendered to sleep, as he knew he would, sooner
or later. It was, of course, the drug that had made him feel like
this, though he did not know it.

There had been too much water for him these past few
days; he hated and feared it as a rabid animal would, and the
mad desire to get as far away from it as possible was very
strong. He must try, he decided, and with a great effort he put
a front hoof forward, then a back one . . . and got no further as
he collapsed onto the ground with a thump. Above, the
hamerkop cried its reedy alarm call and disappeared through
the narrow entrance to its nest.

Kali-Anuka slept dangerously, with all his senses inactive.
Only his breathing indicated that he was alive; only the
sharpest eye of any passing fellow-creature — bird, mammal,
snake or reptile — could have perceived the movement in his
chest as he breathed. Swarms of insects settled on his
recumbent body, gathering on the cuts and grazes scarring his
legs and belly; but he did not stir. Concealed under the tree
cover, no reconnoitring vulture saw him, and, perhaps
because so many predators had already moved to other areas,
away from the flooding, none came near.

He dreamed an animal dream, a fantasy beyond his own
experience. He grew wings, and flew like an eagle over a land
covered with water, but looking down he could see that other
animals walked on the water, calling up to him to help them
escape, to help them become winged, too, and fly away with
him. He flew through dark clouds, but they were made of
thick, viscous mud which stuck to his wing feathers, bringing
him down. Heavier and heavier they became, but he fought
against falling, down and down towards the solid water below.
Then the wings severed from his body, and before he followed
them down he saw all the animals fighting among themselves
to claim them, but they all sank in the water, still calling to
him. Then he, too, fell through the air, but into a soft white
cloud, and there was lush, green pasture on which many

impalas grazed. He heard a voice say, "I have been waiting for you, Kali-Anuka . . . but you have come sooner than I expected." It was the voice of Mwami, and the dream ended.

The storm had broken as night fell, and when Kali-Anuka awoke after his dream, he thought he dreamed still, drowning with the animals he had seen in his flight. He imagined he was lying at the foot of a great waterfall, the rain so pounded him. In reality, his reclining body was half covered in water which swirled about him; but this was not the river, only the accumulation of rain from the blackness above, streaked with lightning flashes.

He pulled himself upright, forcing his body against the lashing rain, relieved at finding himself still living, relieved that his legs supported him now without much pain. His head was clearer, too, though it continued to ache. He began walking, avoiding the broken mound of the hamerkop's nest which had been torn down by the wind out of the fork in the tree. That's half a year's work gone to waste, he thought, bravely whimsical despite his own troubles.

The sharp points of rain stung his skin, almost to the bone, but it did not worry him any more, and he pressed on, moving slowly further and further inland, seeing no familiar features, seeing nothing much at all through the rain. He heard nothing except the cacophonous sounds of the storm — the hissing rain, the wild soughing of the trees, the rushing streams which crossed and recrossed his path following the uneven lie of the land. It seemed to him he walked for half the night, until the intensity of the storm began to wane, and the thunder rolled away on the wind.

Through the lightening gloom, he could see a rising hillock here, a grove of shrubby bloodwood trees there; a cluster of tumbled rocks, a great, partially eroded anthill. But still he did not know where he was.

Suddenly he was conscious of his hunger and paused to crop some mopane leaves. Later, he lay down on a bed of short, spongy grass, ruminating himself into a brief half-sleep.

He stirred at the first, tentative light of dawn, filled his mouth with more leaves and resumed his walking, munching as he went, his nose, eyes and ears alert to any danger, now that something like normal life had returned to the battered valley. A bright orange tiger-snake, black-blotched, slid slenderly across his path, a small lizard held in its fangs; then, with a swift whoosh of powerful wings, a bateleur eagle swooped on the snake, snatched it in its talons and carried it away, all in one smooth, continuous movement. The lizard, released from the fangs of the writhing snake, fell through the air, somersaulting into the mud below, surprised at its survival.

The cycle of life and death had returned to the valley; all was as it should be, on the face of it. But still the Great Valley continued to shrink.

Twice Kali-Anuka caught the unmistakable scent of a pack of wild dogs, but he did not feel threatened as they were hunting upwind from him, and would not pick up his own scent. The presence of traditional enemies of impalas, though far away, reminded him of his recent contact with the Zimikile, and he found it puzzling to compare that experience with the other, when Mwami had died from the wound inflicted by the banging stick, so long ago. But there was another, wider experience, he thought; and it was happening now. For what was all this turmoil going on in the valley, but the evil work of the Zimikile? Perhaps they made the storms too, for all he knew. Yet he could not doubt, looking back on it in all the detail he could remember, that the men on their floating carrier had saved his life, had lifted him from certain drowning in the floods they had created themselves. It made no sense. Or had they known who he was? Had they known of Mwami and the Pambuka, and that he, Kali-Anuka, was Mwami's son and successor? No, he decided, they could not have known of that — and of what importance would it be to them if they had?

He swallowed the wad of cud he had been chewing. Immersed in his thoughts, he had not noticed that the ground had begun to rise sharply; that, perhaps by some mysterious force, he was being guided towards the high ground where Yandika had taken the rest of the herd. He walked on, surprised at such a return of strength to his heavily taxed limbs and body.

If he needed proof of the evil ways of the Zimikile, he told himself, he only had to think of Fura-Uswa, who when he was alive saw with his own eyes the destruction of every one of his kin by both kinds of Zimikile, whether by spear, trap or banging stick. There seemed no reason for it, and perhaps there was none. Then he began to compare the ways of the Zimikile to those of other enemies, if they could be called that. The predators — lions, cheetahs and wild dogs; leopards, hyenas and caracals; the eagles who sometimes preyed on impala lambs — they killed, but only to fill their bellies, to survive and propagate their own kind. This was fair, and when they hunted they used their teeth and claws and strength to kill quickly and decisively. Not like the others, who with their deadly sticks and traps killed quickly only when they were lucky; more often, they inflicted cruel wounds and left the victim to die slowly in his own agonising loneliness. He had never seen an elephant man-trapped, but Mwami told him of one who fought for five days and nights to free himself. When he did, a foreleg was severed below the knee and it was another ten days of screaming pain before the creature was driven mad with torture and drowned himself in the river.

There was another story Mwami told, of one of the Pambuka does who, many years ago, was struck by a black man's spear which pierced deep into her shoulder. She was with lamb, and although she lived many days in almost unbearable pain, weakened with loss of blood, the wound festering and the spear tearing it open with every movement, she survived to see her lamb born, and suckled it while she lay dying, long enough to give it nourishment for its criticial first few days of life.

Yes, Kali-Anuka had learnt much of the ways of men during his short span of life. He nursed no hate for them, for he did not understand their motives. Perhaps there were some good reasons for their evil practices, or perhaps they were not all the same, like those who had pulled him up out of the drowning water — to help him live. The image of the man-face close to his came to him, just before he had felt the sharp stab, as from a thorn, in his rump; he understood even less as he considered the reality of the dam and the flood.

That was enough thinking for one tired impala, he decided. He shook his head, and to help clear his over-burdened mind he gave a muffled snort.

Abruptly, he stopped, his body tensed and his nose tilted up, nostrils working to identify a scent which came and went so quickly he could not establish its source. He knew it was close, but first it came from one direction, then from another. It was distinctly fishy, and he stood rigidly still, waiting for another waft of it, to be sure. But the voice came first, from a flat ledge high above his head.

"So there you are, my friend! Looking like you shouldn't be here at all!"

Tantalika, who had been darting to and fro, circling his old friend, making certain it was indeed he, suddenly confronted Kali-Anuka in characteristic style, not two otter-lengths away from his front hooves.

"I'm here through no thanks to you," Kali-Anuka said rather peevishly. "Why didn't you come back to the waterfall? I waited until morning."

"Well, as you know, I was — er, my attention was directed elsewhere." Tantalika's eyes shone at the memory. "But truly," he went on, "Vutuka and I didn't notice the night passing so quickly, and of course by first light when we came back, you'd gone. Now, my friend, you look about ready for the vultures — and what's that thing on your left ear?"

Kali-Anuka did not know what he meant, so he ignored the question, and the otter did not ask it again.

They moved close under the ledge, Tantalika keeping one eye on an old antbear hole nearby, ready to use it instantly for refuge in case of danger. Then Kali-Anuka told him of all that had happened to him since they had parted, and when he came to describe what he called his 'rescue' by the Zimikile he was surprised that his companion did not react incredulously.

"Ah," he said, knowingly, "I saw them, probably the same ones, with the zebras. And a very curious thing it was, too."

"Zebras? What zebras?"

Then Tantalika related the story, and when he had finished, they both remained silent, deep in their own thoughts.

"It's quite clear," the otter said at last, "that these Zimikile don't want us animals to die . . ."

". . . to drown in the floods they've created," said Kali-Anuka, completing the sentence for him.

"But it must be others who have made the dam, and those we saw are different, and good."

"I shall never forget," mused Kali-Anuka, "the look on that pale one's face — although it wasn't really so pale — as I lay, half-dead and ready for death, on the floating carrier. He had such a strange face, as they all have, but a look came over it and showed in his eyes, that I couldn't mistake. It was like . . . like the softness in Kusomona's eyes when we're together, and I've done something to please her."

There was another quiet moment, and Tantalika remembered Vutuka and the look that sometimes came into her eyes.

Then Kali-Anuka shook himself, with a feeling of guilt.

"May the good Fura-Uswa forgive me, but I haven't yet asked you of Kusomona, and Swilila . . . where are all the Pambuka now? And has Kusomona dropped her lamb — is she well?"

"Ah yes!" said Tantalika, and to Kali-Anuka's delight he told of the birth of the young Mwami-Mupati. "But I fear for him more than for the others. They're in a place high above the water now, but soon it may become another island, and then there'll be swimming to be done — and none that I know of are able to swim for more than the width of a small stream."

"Then we must go to them at once!"

"No, Kali-Anuka. You're in no condition to attempt a long swim, for the flood has already deepened since they walked across. You must remain here until you've got back your strength, and then we'll go to them. If you reached them today, you couldn't do much, whatever happened."

A smile came into Kali-Anuka's eyes.

"Oh yes," he said softly. "I could die with them."

"Tsss!" hissed Tantalika, "a fat lot of good that would do!"

"It would make things easier for them. Don't forget, I've nearly drowned two or three times already, and I know how it feels. It must be the worst kind of death . . . if one is alone. Oh, you wouldn't know about that," he added impatiently, "when so much of your life is spent in the water."

Tantalika flicked his tail angrily.

"I think you're mad — and I'm not surprised after what you've been through. But if you could see yourself, you'd know that unless you rest, and feed — get some flesh back to cover your bones — you couldn't even walk to the water, let alone get across it. Please," he begged, "wait for a day or two. You'll be more use to them alive than dead."

"And if they all die, meanwhile?"

"One survivor — and the leader of the Pambuka, at that — will be better than none at all. If the rest of the herd all go, you could still start up a new one."

"Not without Kusomona and Mupati; not without Swilila."

Perhaps the thought of them brought a new resolve to him, a new strength and purpose, for a shudder travelled through his body from head to tail, and he stepped forward in short, bucking leaps, almost knocking Tantalika over, spattering him with mud.

"I'm going, Tantalika, and you must show me the way," he called over his shoulder, and the otter came up and trotted along beside him, muttering protests through his whiskers.

They went on through the mud, ever climbing, and then

the trees grew thicker, and Kali-Anuka had to slow his pace as
he followed the otter through dense bush along the rocky
hillside. It was well into the afternoon when they broke
through to clearer ground, which sloped down until their path
ran out, where the encroaching waters had circled inland from
the river. It was near where Tantalika had taken the others
across before, but he knew the water would be deep, and now
selected a deeper, but narrower expanse for them to cross.

"Well, here we are," he announced. "Do you think you
can swim across to that mound, between those two trees over
there?"

Kali-Anuka, his front hooves already in the water,
looked. It was not very far, but he could see the hazards. Many
trees grew out of the water, the shorter ones with their
branches under the surface to snare him if he were not careful.
It was unlikely that crocodiles would have moved into the area
yet, and even if they had, Tantalika would be beside him to
act as a distraction. Not far distant he could see, in among the
foliage of a mopane, a gathering of vervet monkeys clinging
desperately by their hands and tails to the branches, plainly
panic-stricken, and unable to decide whether to remain where
they were or to drop into the water and swim to safety. They
must have been debating this problem for a long time, for the
trunk of the tree was already half-submerged. As Kali-Anuka
and Tantalika watched, a big male, clearly the leader,
suddenly made the long awaited choice, and leapt out of the
tree, falling feet first into the water. He was followed by many
more as all but the most timid dropped in after him. Babies
clung with their arms around their mothers' stomachs; some
held fast, but many relaxed their grip on impact with the
water and were lost. The adults swam on, dog-paddling,

moving at a fair speed, but all in different directions, few with any chance of reaching shore before exhaustion overtook them.

"Just look at the fools!" said Tantalika. "They're good swimmers, but they're so full of panic they're throwing away their chances. Idiots!"

"I wish we could do something to help them, poor things," Kali-Anuka said, with compassion. "Come on, Tantalika — let's get in among them, quickly, and perhaps they'll follow us across."

He started forward, but as the water slapped against his white belly, Tantalika, in a rapid movement, swam out in front of him.

"Wait!" he said, treading water. "Don't be as stupid as those monkeys, Kali-Anuka — wait a while and rest. You're already just about done — on your last legs, may I say — so for Fura-Uswa's sake rest, and get your strength back. Rest, just long enough for that cloud to pass across the sun. Then we'll go."

Kali-Anuka raised his eyes to the sky. A great white cloud had just obscured the sun, moving across slowly; it would be a long time before it passed.

"No, we must go now," he said, "because later I may falter, and not go at all."

So ignoring the otter's advice, he settled in the water and paddled away towards the mound on the other side, which would bring him to the foot of the hills on which Tantalika had told him the others were. Unable to stop him, jabbering protests at his foolishness, the otter turned and swam ahead, slipping underwater now and then to check that the way was clear of entanglements, keeping his eyes open for crocodiles, whether he was above or below the surface.

By now the monkeys — those who still had the strength to swim — had scattered far and wide; the rest had disappeared, or floated lifeless on the surface.

A sudden tug at his short tail startled Kali-Anuka when he was half-way across. He dared not turn his head, and swam on, paying as little attention to the slight drag on his progress as he could. He tried to attract Tantalika's eye, but the otter was far ahead, weaving through the many obstacles. Something had attached itself to his tail, there was no doubt about that, but the pull remained constant, so he ceased to worry about it, thinking it was perhaps a small piece of debris. What concerned him more was when, as he passed under a bough of a tree, so close that he was afraid his horns might catch in it, a writhing skein of spitting cobras fell, sliding over his muzzle as they did so. There must have been six, or more; one of them had time to spit its twin jets of venom at him before it twisted away through the water, but fortunately the poison missed his eyes. Had it not, blindness might have followed rapidly.

Soon he was near the two trees Tantalika had pointed out earlier, and his hind hooves touched solid ground. Still he could feel the pull on his tail, and as he saw Tantalika glide out of the water ahead of him, climb ashore to sit awaiting his arrival, he heard him laugh through his chattering teeth.

"You've put one over on the Zimikile this time!" he called across the intervening stretch of water. "The great Kali-Anuka, saver of lives! I wouldn't be surprised if they'd like to have you as one of their carriers!"

When Kali-Anuka, once again so near utter exhaustion, managed to climb ashore, he felt the pull on his tail relax. He turned his head, wearily, to catch a glimpse of a young vervet monkey scrambling away into the bush, as fast as he could.

"And he didn't even say thank you!" laughed Tantalika.

Although he wanted to, Kali-Anuka could not join in the otter's laughter. Out of the water, he swayed on his legs, then with a great effort put one before the other, lifting his limp, dripping body up the steep bank, almost crawling. He collapsed and rolled over on his side amid a tangle of bracken. His eyes closed, but before he drifted away into unconsciousness Tantalika ran over to him and spoke in his ear.

"Listen, Kali-Anuka," he said. "Do not try to move. I'm going now to bring the others to you. Vutuka will come first to watch over you. Do you understand me, my dear friend?"

There was no laughter in his voice now, only deep concern.

Tantalika pressed his ear close to the other's mouth, the voice was so quiet.

"Yes . . . I hear you. But it's all over, Tantalika . . . all over . . . for me . . ."

His voice trailed away in a long, breathing sigh, and he lay perfectly still.

Without a backward glance, but with a heavy heart, the otter ran off and up the wooded hillside, moving fast. And as he hurried towards the hill beyond, where Vutuka and the five impalas waited, he called upon Fura-Uswa to protect Kali-Anuka, to let him live the life he deserved, this bravest of all impalas, whose bravery had nevertheless clouded his wisdom.

When Kali-Anuka opened his eyes it was night and the stars shone from a black, velvety sky. There was no moon, but a light breeze stirred the leaves of the two mopane trees near him; he could hear familiar, nocturnal animal noises, but they seemed far away, as though they belonged to another world. At the moment of waking he did not feel refreshed; the aches all over his body and in his head and legs were so great that when he tried to move, only to lift his head, a flood of pain overwhelmed him and he lay still again.

He did not think the others would come until morning if, indeed, they came at all, for he knew there would be a high concentration of animals in the area now that the floods had reached so far, and many would be seeking easy prey. But

Vutuka came. He was unaware of her coming until, in his half-sleep, he felt a tickling sensation under an ear, and then a quiet little squeak. At first he thought some small rodent, a mouse or a shrew, was curiously investigating this new, living feature which had encroached on its territory. But when he heard another squeak, some tiny grunts which came astonishingly close to pronouncing his name, he moved his eyes and saw the dark shape of the she-otter sitting beside him in the curve of his neck. He could not acknowledge her presence by word or movement, but she must have understood, because she stroked his mouth with her fingers and nipped his ear tenderly, as if telling him she knew he could not speak.

Several times during the remainder of the night she scuttled away, silently, to check on stealthy sounds in the bush around them. She could have done little to protect either herself or Kali-Anuka, had any intruder intended harm, except to lead whoever it was away from the powerless impala. But on no occasion was this necessary. Once, just before dawn, she slipped down the slope into the dark water to search for food but found nothing to satisfy her hunger.

It was not until the sun had lifted clear into the pale morning sky, and a warm breeze strengthened, rustling the leaves about him, that Kali-Anuka became fully conscious. He could feel, through the dancing leaves, the warmth of sunlight on his body, but still he felt no physical sensations within it; he could not move a muscle, though his ears flicked against the flies, his nostrils twitched, and his eyes could see all around him.

Vutuka, nearby, reached up to a low-hanging mopane branch, snapped off a leafy twig with her fingers, and offered it to him, holding the leaves close to his mouth. Although he tried hard, he had no strength to take them. She persevered, and after a long time he opened his mouth wide enough to nibble at a leaf or two.

This was how they found him when they came, all five impalas and Tantalika. There was no great show of emotion, although first Swilila, then Kusomona, sniffed at him to make sure it was indeed he. Reassured (despite the small thing attached to his ear, which puzzled them), they licked and nuzzled him as he painfully chomped at the cud in his mouth. He could show no joy when Kusomona pushed a reluctant Mupati close to his nose, but inwardly a glow of pride spread from his faintly beating heart through his veins, and for one brief, exquisite moment, all his pain vanished.

Fortunately, there was plenty of good browse near where Kali-Anuka lay; fortunately, too, Tantalika reckoned at least one more day would pass before the flood reached his stricken friend. There was nothing the otters or the depleted herd could do to hasten Kali-Anuka's recovery, except to feed him with moist leaves, and let nature do the healing. This she did very well (perhaps with Fura-Uswa's help), and on the morning of the next day, as the first streak of dawn extinguished the light from the stars, one by one, he slowly sat up on his haunches, rested for a while, then levered himself up to stand, shakily, and stagger a few paces towards Kusomona who sat, half-reclining, with her lamb beside her. He filled his mouth with leaves, and lay at her side.

Already he had filled out a little. His bones no longer ridged his skin as they had done before. The old shine of his coat had not yet returned, but most of the open sores from thorns, and the tears on his belly, had scabbed over; the flies had left him to seek more rewarding sources of food.

Through the day he continued to ache terribly, all over,

but after each period of rest, lying full length on the ground, with Kusomona and Mupati nearby, there was less pain each time he rose to fill his mouth with the nourishing mopane leaves or the reedy grass which grew abundantly.

On the fourth day, when the sky became dull and overcast with rainclouds flying low, he pronounced himself ready to move from this place to the haven the others had reached before, on higher ground.

"And about time, too," Tantalika said lightly.

He and Vutuka had just come out of the water, now quite close to where the impalas were grouped.

"By tomorrow the flood will be here, where you stand," stated the otter. "Already it's washing away the mess you left where you were lying for so long, keeping us all worrying and waiting."

Kali-Anuka's eyes smiled at him.

"All right," he said, "we can go now. But one point I must make first," he added sternly, looking straight at Yandika. "Until I say otherwise, you must remain the leader. I am still weak in body, and my senses are dulled — we must all rely on you, Yandika, to lead us until I am myself again."

Tantalika remained silent, and Silulimi gave a little snort which Kali-Anuka did not hear.

But Yandika heard it.

"No," he said, "I don't think I . . . I can't . . ."

"You must do as I say," Kali-Anuka interrupted, "and that's the last order I give you, or any of you, until we've reached the place you have told me about, and I am well again."

The trek over the hill was uneventful; they went down into the valley which was little more than a fold between the two hills. Until mid-morning Kali-Anuka could not take more than a few faltering steps at a time before he was forced to rest, while the others waited for him patiently. Later, each resting period became shorter, and every walk became longer, until by noon they were half-way across the shallow valley, and a refreshing, cooling drizzle of rain descended on them from the low, misty clouds. Progress slowed in the afternoon as they climbed the side of the next hill towards the summit and their destination. Yandika wisely led them at an angle across the hillside, for although this increased the distance covered, it put less of a strain on Kali-Anuka. It was not, in fact, Yandika's own idea, but whispered advice from Tantalika, which the other gladly accepted.

By late afternoon they were all on the broad, flat top of the hill, and although Kali-Anuka could not have taken another step, for all his aches and pains had returned, he was pleased with what he saw. He lay on short, palatable turf, while the others once again luxuriated among all the good things they found in what was to be their home range for a long time.

Seeing him alone, Tantalika came and sat before him, as he had often done.

"Well, old friend, you are indeed the son of Mwami," he said. "And to tell you the truth, I can't tell you how greatly I admire you."

"I owe you my life, a hundred times over . . . we all do," countered Kali-Anuka, "and there's nothing you can say will better that! But," he went on, "I have the feeling, by the tone of your voice, that you are not staying with us?"

The otter laughed, baring his chattering teeth.

"You've regained your wisdom, Kali-Anuka, and it equals your bravery! Yes — I must take Vutuka away, and return to our normal lives. The time is close for us to start a family, and we must find a suitable place, where there is plenty of river food."

"But now the river has gone, where will you find it ?"

"That may be a problem," Tantalika conceded, "though there are other rivers — and even a good stream will do. It may take us a long time, and far away. That is why we must go now, without delay."

Kali-Anuka bowed his head.

"We'll miss you — both of you," he said, thinking of Vutuka's care when he had been unable to help himself.

"This place," said Tantalika, "should be safe from the Zimikile flood, unless they are planning to drown the whole world. But for a while it may not be safe from your other enemies — when we were here before I found many of them, and there will be much hunting. You must be careful, extra careful, especially at the drinking-pool, which is known to the others — Yandika will show you where it is."

Tantalika dropped down from his standing position, and did something he had never done before, even with Mwami. He nuzzled Kali-Anuka's nose, and gently bit his ear.

"I'm going now with Vutuka," he said, struggling with his words, "and if we can find the rest of the herd we will guide them here — if they're not too far away — so that the Pambuka is whole again. If we cannot find them, then this must be our farewell."

"We may never meet again — is that what you mean?" Kali-Anuka was deeply moved.

Tantalika edged away from his friend and, poised on all fours to hurry off to join Vutuka, he left Kali-Anuka with his last message.

"We shall meet again, I think. But only Fura-Uswa will give the answer to that!"

And he was gone.

10

IN man's measurements of length and time, the closing of the last gaps in the Kariba dam wall caused the Zambezi river to rise nearly twenty feet in twenty-four hours; by the end of the first week it had risen another thirty feet, and after two weeks more, all along the valley, it had gone up sixty-five feet. Within two months, by the beginning of February 1959, the river had swelled into an irregular shaped lake, five or six miles wide in places. Some rivers which formerly had flowed into it ceased to exist.

Some of the islands which formed as the water rose, disappeared quickly, together with every living thing on them which was unable to swim, or fly to the temporary safety of even higher ground. Other islands shrank only so far, and then eventually became permanent features in the lake. But there were those which were to shrink slowly, inch by inch, before they were completely submerged.

It was on one of these last that the remaining six impalas of the Pambuka herd had sought refuge, and made themselves at home, although it was not an island as yet. This new home range was rich in browse, although good grazing was patchy. There was a wide variety of trees, but few of the leaves were palatable to them; they liked the thin, leathery leaves of the bushwillows, and the pale green leaves of the coca tree best, though both were unfamiliar to them. The mopanes were in scattered thickets, but they were plentiful.

Had the herd not split up on that day when the Zimikile carrier had been heard from the river, it would have numbered forty-two, an increase of only one since Kali-Anuka's birth over three years before. But when, one day, after the last heavy rains were over, the breakaway contingent came through a fringe thicket of red bushwillows, nonchalantly as though it had never left, it comprised only three rams and nine does. There were no young.

Their leader, a two-year-old with one horn which twisted oddly over his left ear (hence he had been named Teketa), told a strange story.

After they had panicked and stupidly followed the terror-stricken ram, they had not gone far before they splashed across a shallow stream which coursed along a wide, sandy bed. The ground rose sharply on the other side, and when they were in among the trees at the top of the slope they were no longer frightened and in a few moments were quietly browsing as if nothing at all had happened. But when the storm broke that evening, and they huddled together under the trees, their fear returned and stayed with them all through the thundering fury of the rain-soaked night. In the morning, without discussion, they moved out from under the trees and started down the steep slope, all calmer now and wanting to return to those they had left the day before. When they came to the stream it was no longer only hoof-deep and gently flowing; it was a surging torrent which no impala living would ever venture to cross.

At first none was seriously concerned, until, after two days, although the force of the stream diminished, the level rose even higher; they realised that unless they found another route they could not hope to get back. It did not take them long to discover that the area they were occupying was a narrow strip, and surrounded by water too deep for them to cross at any point.

Leaderless, and although they did not know it, with only enough food to last a short time, they were frightened and very confused. It was Teketa who rallied them, brushing aside feeble protests from the ram who had led them away; it was Teketa who appointed himself their leader, and urged them to make the best of circumstances until they could escape when the waters fell. But, of course, the waters continued to rise.

In one way they were lucky. The island was small — no more than ten impala leaps wide, and thirty long — but no other animals shared it with them except for a large number of rodents, a few nightapes, and a single, bad-tempered honey-badger, none of whom would offer serious competition for the limited food available. There was not much of anything left when, several days later, they heard again the sound which had brought them there in the first place. From this point, Teketa's memory was confused, a mixture of impressions, of things heard, smelled and seen, and it was difficult for Kali-Anuka and the others to piece the story together. Teketa's companions were not of much help, for they, too, could only recall disconnected sensations of what had taken place.

The words came in short bursts from Teketa, and three or four of the others.

"We ran, with the Zimikile running behind us, shouting and beating branches . . ." said one.

". . . we leapt and ran, some fell dead with shock. We were so scared," said another.

"Some leapt into the water and drowned," a third said.

"Suddenly we were all tangled up among hanging vines, or something like that, and the Zimikile came at us."

"A doe — couldn't see who it was — broke her leg . . . I heard a Zimikile stick go bang, and she was dead."

"We kicked at them with our hooves . . ."

". . . and ripped at them with our horns," added a ram.

"There was a lot of blood . . ."

". . . and then our legs were tied, tightly."

"A tall Zimikile threw water over us . . . he wore a strange, high head-covering." Teketa had noticed this.

"They carried us to the water . . ."

". . . and put us on the carrier-creatures . . ."

". . . the smells, the noise, were horrible."

And then, through the hubbub of voices, Teketa's memory came clearer, and he took up the tale.

"All of us here," he said, "were carried over the water, then lifted on to land. We couldn't move, because of the vines on our legs. Then, one by one, our legs were freed and we were pushed away by the Zimikile — who when you are close to them give off a most peculiar scent — and we were all together again. But many were left on the island to starve to death, or drown as the flood rose higher. Those who died when the Zimikile chased us were lucky, perhaps, to go so quickly."

Kali-Anuka interrupted.

"So how did you find us? Did you come from far away?"

"We were, indeed, far away, but I cannot tell you where. Tantalika came one night, with his she-otter, and told us you were at this place. His directions were very clear — very clear indeed — but we were lost many times, and it has taken us through three full moons to come. I told him there were others left behind on the island; he was very sad about that."

"Why didn't he bring you himself? He said he would."

"I don't know," answered Teketa. "He was in a great hurry, and said something about Vutuka I couldn't understand."

Kali-Anuka smiled.

"Nothing else?" he asked.

There was a long pause while Teketa searched his memory.

Tell "Ah . . . yes!" he said. "I remember now. He gave me a message for you. 'Tell Kali-Anuka that we were right about the Zimikile.' You would understand that, he said."

When Teketa and the others had moved off, Kali-Anuka pondered the otter's words. What had he meant? He thought about some of their last conversations . . . when was it they had talked about the Zimikile? Then he remembered. It was when they had met soon after his experience with them in the water, and on the carrier-creature; they had agreed on the possibility that, perhaps, not all Zimikile are evil. Was that it? Judging by what he had heard from Teketa and his party, it did not seem so.

But then he thought to himself: had those Zimikile not come to the little island, would Teketa and his companions be here now? Would they not have drowned, or soon starved to death, when all the food had gone? Would he, Kali-Anuka, still be alive if *his* Zimikile had not lifted him, so close to death, from the deepening river, and brought him safely to dry land? So, he reasoned, there are those who wish to destroy, and another kind who wish to preserve. But, as he had done before, he gave up trying to work out what the motives of either could be.

"And how, in Fura-Uswa's name, can one tell the difference?" he asked himself aloud.

There was another event a few days later which gladdened the heart of Kali-Anuka (and the other four rams, too), when seven does rejoined the herd. They told an equally garbled

story, all talking at once, just as Teketa's party had. The same group of Zimikile had returned to the island, driven them into the water, hoisted them on to the carrier, and taken them to the main shore. Soon after their legs had been untied, and they had run off into the bush, they had found Tantalika and Vutuka waiting, impatient to be off on their own pleasure. Assured that no more impalas remained alive on the island, Tantalika directed them to the main herd, and both otters ran off with hardly a word of farewell.

So, Kali-Anuka thought once again, he was right about the meaning of the otter's message. Convinced of the good intentions of the Zimikile, Tantalika had waited for more survivors to be brought from the island, despite his haste to be away; and his belief had been proved correct.

Again Kali-Anuka was faced with the same difficulty, and returned to his earlier self-questioning: how can one tell the difference between good and bad? Do the good ones smell different? Look different? Should he tell his impalas not to be frightened of any Zimikile who come near — or only some? But which? He remembered Mwami's death, the scent and the look of the killers; the only way to tell them apart then was that one was pale, the other dark. Both were bad, no doubt about that, unless they had been on the hunt for food. But that could not be, for they had gone away and not returned to take Mwami's body. Therefore, looks had nothing to do with it. It was too much for him. Perhaps, one day, he would have the answers; meanwhile he would continue to work at re-establishing the unity of his decimated Pambuka clan, adapting its members to their new habitat which, come to think of it, had been well chosen by Tantalika — unless, of course, it too became an island.

There were also the pleasures of the rutting season to anticipate; he had fully recovered from his earlier trials, and was back in full health.

They all missed the daily trails down to the river which they had had when in their old home range. It had never been far

away, making a pleasant change
to amble down to the little strip
of beach to drink, or relish their
own special grass. Now there
was no river, no sweet grass to
go to; only a great expanse of
water as far as their weak eyes
could reach, broken in places
with the crowns of trees which
had not yet been totally submerged. It was a long way to
travel for a drink, when all they

had to do was walk through the small forest of bushwillows
and acacias, across a shadowy glade of coca trees inter-
mingled with mopanes, down into a steep fold which formed a
narrow valley. There, a thin stream trickled into a pool, and
out on the other side. As the rainless days set in, the stream
ceased to flow, its sandy bed drying quickly under the warm
sun; but the pool remained, although the level dropped with
evaporation, and from the thirsts of the many creatures who
shared it.

Tantalika had been right, as usual. There were many
animals in the area who preyed on impalas, but perhaps
because of the high population of other, smaller antelope —
duikers, grysbok and the klipspringers up in the many rocky
kopjes — who were easier meat, the predators waxed fat and
lazy, seldom bothering with the Pambuka impalas. One
female was taken by a leopard early in the season, another by
a pack of ten wild dogs, but that was all; by impala standards,
loss of life this winter was minimal.

The annual rut came and went as usual, without serious
casualties, and Yandika, for the first time, challenged another
male for mating rights, choosing the dangle-horned Teketa.
He chose deliberately, for his eyes had been on a pale, slim
doe who had paid much attention to Teketa since she had
reached maturity a short time before. With only one effective
horn, Teketa would be easy to vanquish, he decided. They
battled out of sight of all the others — though not out of

earshot, for their roars could be heard for miles around — and
Yandika was glad they did, in the end. After brief, preliminary

skirmishes, advancing towards each other in turn, their
hooves raising little clouds of dust as they twisted and turned,
awaiting an opportunity for a lightning thrust with lowered
horns, Teketa suddenly side-swiped with the tip of his
malformed horn. It struck Yandika sharply above and between
the eyes, drawing blood which trickled down into each eye,
blinding him. It was all over for Yandika, who withdrew to
hide himself in the dark depths of the jesse, and Teketa leapt
happily away, roaring and snorting triumphantly, to claim his
mate.

Up until the moon of Wasinkula, in July, when the leaves
of many trees began to fall, the survivors of the Pambuka, now
only sixteen, had lived well off the grasses and woody browse,
the fruit of the trees of their new territory. But Kali-Anuka
was becoming increasingly aware that soon they would have
to be on the move again. Hopefully, it would not have to be far
away, but with the approach of the driest part of the season, in
the spring, together with the high concentration of vegetarian
animals in the area close to the pool, there would be little left
to eat.

One day, with Kusomona and Mwami-Mupati, Kali-
Anuka set out to reconnoitre the perimeter of his new domain,
to find, perhaps, a better place outside it. They probed
beyond the border, but found nowhere more attractive. They
encountered many animals — small groups of buffalo, eland,

zebra, kudu and waterbuck. Troops of baboons watched them pass, pausing in their search for lizards, scorpions and beetles on the ground; vervet monkeys screamed at them for no reason at all. Solitary, or in pairs, they saw bushbuck and warthogs; there were others they did not see — duikers and grysbok, who mostly lay up in daylight — but he knew there were many. There were no elephants, though a large herd had visited the drinking-pool daily until a few days before. Evidence of their recent presence abounded — a winding path from the pool into the thick surrounding bush; tall trees lying flat, uprooted for a mouthful of twigs beyond their normal reach; small shrubs wrenched out of the ground with their trunks, the dusty remains littering wide areas at intervals along the trail.

A sound behind them made Kali-Anuka and Kusomona turn their heads, and there was Mupati mock-challenging another young ram of his own age. They stood watching the two enjoying their game, flinging up the dust under their little hooves, skirmishing with their straight, uncurved horns, further and further away towards an outcrop of rocks. Suddenly, from behind the rocks, there was a flash of a white tail, and a wild dog ran swiftly from its cover towards the playing impalas. It was clearly diseased, thin and emaciated, desperate for food. Separated from its pack, its solitary hunting had met with little success for a long time, and now it had grown so weak it was no great threat to any healthy prey. Kali-Anuka leapt forward, cutting across the dog's intended path, making it swerve sharply away from the youngsters. Unable to control the movements of its legs, the dog tumbled among the rocks and made off, whining pitifully in its frustration, leaving its offensive odour hanging on the air.

The young rams, unaware of the danger, thinking Kali-Anuka was ready to join their game, separated and ran to him, tiny horns lowered. He stood his ground, and they prodded at his flank gently, and then, as they walked together to the waiting Kusomona, other impalas bounded across the littered ground from the jesse nearby.

There were three rams and a doe. They came, they said,

from a small herd with territory not far away, down by the
water. There were questions and answers from both sides,
and then their leader spoke to Kali-Anuka of his fears about
the ever-rising level of the flood. Did he think it would ever
stop? Would it be wise to move away from here, while they
still could? But Kali-Anuka could not help him, for he did not
know the answers. They parted company in the hope of
meeting again, and Mupati looked longingly back at his friend
as he trotted off at the side of the doe, his mother.

It was not until later that Kali-Anuka recalled having
heard the voice of the leader before. He tried to place it, and
then remembered Kwizima, whom he had talked with on the
other side of the river, by the waterfall. How, he wondered,
had Kwizima managed to be here — on the wrong side of the
river? He shook his head, and moved on with his charges; it
was none of his business, so he forgot about it.

Soon, from higher ground, the trio looked down on the
shallow valley they had travelled over with Tantalika. As Kali-
Anuka recognised it, he snorted, and tapped a front hoof on
the ground.

"Do you see, Kusomona?" he said, concerned. "Do you
see what is happening . . . again?"

The valley between the hills had gone. It was under water
now, and they could see the long, low hill on the far side was an
island.

Kusomona spoke softly.

"Is this never to end? Is all the world to drown?"

They gazed at the scene in silence.

"What do we do now, Kali? Where do we go?"

He did not answer. They turned away to follow the
trail back, Mupati bounding ahead, blissfully unaware of his
father's problems, while Kusomona stayed close beside her
mate, with watchful eyes ever on her son.

Kali-Anuka walked slowly, his head bowed in deep
thought, and except for the wholeness of his horns, he could
have been a replica of the long-dead Mwami.

The first rains were still to come, and as the ground became drier under the hot, penetrating sun, much of the remaining vegetation on the trees and bushes withered and died. What was left became less and less as it was cropped, and there was green only on the highest branches of the trees.

For a time the great concentration of animals moved closer around the vicinity of the drinking-pool, but soon, as the food became scarcer and scarcer, most gave up in exasperation, and went off in search of better pastures — if they could find them.

Kali-Anuka would not listen to those who thought the Pambuka should follow the example of the others. No, he said, we have water, and will not be without food for long, for at the time of Tundwa fresh leaves will start forming on the trees, and there will be new grass sprouting from the soil. This is a good place, he said; it is our home now, and there is no reason to leave it; there is nowhere better, I know. He did not tell them that he and Kusomona had seen the flood still rising, but he could not believe it could come much higher; if it did, then Kusomona was right and the whole world would drown, with nothing destined to live on. So they would stay, and that was his last word on the subject. Until, as he led them to the drinking-pool on a cool mid-morning, he saw that the sand of the dry bed of the stream was scarred with rivulets of clear, clean water. None commented on this to him; perhaps they had not noticed. But on the next day the rivulets had merged into a stream which flowed stronger and fuller than he had ever seen it before. All saw it this time; they could not fail to. Even Mupati ran to his mother to ask if, somewhere, the rains had come again. Most of the others did not know what to make of it; only Kali-Anuka could understand the true and exact significance of a dry stream which suddenly burst into life — when for days no clouds of any kind, let alone rainclouds, had marred the clean face of the sky from horizon to horizon, day and night. But Yandika and Teketa suspected the truth. Had Kali-Anuka's wisdom been affected by his earlier experiences, and his mind not recovered as his body had? So asked Teketa of Yandika; they no longer bore one another malice.

"That could be so," Yandika answered, "but he is our leader, and we must trust him. Remember what happened last time, when you didn't trust me!"

It took only ten days for the stream to be transformed into a river, and the drinking-pool to widen into a lake. A great assortment of animals crossed the water before it became too wide and deep, while others headed off southwards to look for a safer habitat. But still Kali-Anuka waited, and the others — even Kusomona — began to question further his obstinacy, and now to his face.

"Trust me as you trusted Mwami," he said to them. "I have good reason to keep you here, and when the time comes I will tell you what it is."

So they trusted him, although the grumbling and the words of censure continued behind his back. He was not sure why he had said this to them, but two or three times of late he had felt, dimly at the back of his mind, the certainty of safe deliverance, a strong premonition that by remaining here, he and the Pambuka were taking the right course. There were no events to substantiate this thought, until one day the steady, droning hum of a Zimikile flying-creature was heard, from far away across the lake. As it came closer, the hum became a roar as the creature flew in low over the trees. Kali-Anuka and several others caught sight of it as it flashed through clear sky, visible through the topmost branches of the trees, and roared away with a deafening crescendo of sound which scattered the herd, and all other animals, in panic. It returned to pass over and over again.

So, although the creature was over their heads only briefly, the impalas were badly frightened; all except Kali-Anuka. He was able to accept the visitation as tangible hope, reasoning that if the Zimikile were riding in the flying-creature. they must be looking for something — and what else but for impalas and other animals?

That night he had a dream, and he dreamed of a Zimikile.

The moon of Bimbe was near its fullness, and there was magic in the air. The moon hung yellow and low over the trees, pouring a great flood of warm light into the glade where Kali-Anuka and his small herd rested. He was partly hidden from the others by the woven gossamer threads of spiders' webs, layer upon layer of them, stretched across the thorny branches of an acacia bush. There was no breeze to stir the silken threads, but points of moonlight danced back and forth, and he stared, fascinated, until he was mesmerised into sleep, though his eyes remained open, seeing nothing. A picture formed in his mind. It had come to him before, but it had been real then. The Zimikile eyes looked down at him, and reflected even more kindness and love than before. He spoke, but his mouth did not move. In a strange language, yet one that Kali-Anuka understood, he said:

"You are a very special impala — to all impalas, and to me. When I come with my friends to your island, do not be frightened, for no harm will come to you, or any of your herd. Remember my words — do not be frightened, and all will be well . . ."

That was all. The Zimikile face dissolved away, and in its place Kali-Anuka's seeing eyes looked upon the sparkling, webbed curtains which hung on the acacia bush. He was more certain than ever now that his decision to stay was the right one.

The dry August winds swept across the territory, day after day, lifting the dust off the impoverished ground and snatching away the few leaves remaining on some of the trees. There was little left to eat now, and when Teketa and Yandika came to their leader one day to tell him there was water all around, Kali-Anuka began to have niggling doubts about his own wisdom, of his dream-message. As he looked at them, and the rest of the herd which stood motionless and dejected amid the clouds of billowing dust and leaves, he felt saddened that all the trials they had gone through, separately or together, should have come to this; that all the brave attempts to survive should, perhaps, come to nothing but slow, starving death. The condition of his Pambuka was pitiful — they all,

even his own Mupati, his Kusomona and his mother Swilila,
were thin, their faces pinched, their coats dull under the grey
dust. It could not be long before one, then another and more,
would fall for want of food, unable to summon the strength to
rise again. Then they would become meat for the scavengers,
and their bones would be picked clean by the vultures and the
ants until nothing else remained. He shuddered.

He went with the two young rams to see for himself what
they had seen, and they did not have to go far before his fears
were confirmed. They were, indeed, on an island, and it was a
very small one. They stood together on a rocky ledge, the
highest point they could find, and all round them was water,
studded with the now familiar half-submerged trees — water
reaching in all directions as far as their eyes could see. It
would not be long, Kali-Anuka thought, before his faith in the
Zimikile will be proved one way or the other.

Teketa interrupted his reverie.

"If you changed your mind now," he said, and his words
sounded almost insulting, "it would be too late. We are near

the end, Kali-Anuka. There can be no escape this time, for not even you could swim so far."

"And where could we go?" asked Yandika. "There's nothing but water."

Under the whistling of the wind and the dry rustling of the trees came another sound, so faint at first that none really noticed it. They turned from the depressing scene, and began to walk slowly down the trail, back to the rest of the herd. But Kali-Anuka suddenly stopped, raising his head high, his ears twisting to catch the sound which now rose above the wind.

"Listen," he said, as the others caught up with him. "Listen carefully . . . what sound other than the wind do you hear?"

They both paused to listen, turning their heads from side to side, from back to front, seeking the direction from which it came.

"You think as I do, Kali-Anuka," said Teketa. "We have both heard it before, even if Yandika hasn't."

"Tell me what you think, then."

"A Zimikile carrier-creature, on the water."

"There is no doubt about it," Kali-Anuka agreed, and a hint of a smile came into his eyes. Then he added, musingly: "Perhaps we shall live, after all."

11

A TRIO of African skimmers flew over a shoal of small fish which were just below the surface of the broadening lake, dipping their flat bills into the water, snapping up a fish each time with unerring accuracy. Suddenly distracted, they flew up in alarm, their long wings carrying them, swiftly, high out of harm's way.

Below, the thirty-foot steel launch chugged steadily along the old course of the river, its blunt bow thrusting through the dark blue swell, which heaved on either side of it. Three small boats, each with an outboard motor canted over the stern, pitched and plunged behind, following without choice, towed by the parent craft. On this were four game rangers, a veterinarian and sixteen black helpers; the smaller boats carried ten or eleven black men on each.

It was hot out on the lake that morning; the rangers and the vet sat stripped to their waists under the canopy which covered the deck from the wheel-house to the stern. The others — the assorted Mashona, Matabele and Batonka tribesmen — found patches of shade where they could.

There was little space to spare. All over the deck was a collection of gear and equipment: rolls of game nets, stout poles already sharpened at the ends, sledge-hammers, balls of strong twine, axes and shovels. Sacks contained wooden pegs, mallets and, of all things, old nylon stockings. Forward of the stubby mast, the deck was covered with several sizes of metal, or rough wooden cages; on top of them was a neatly folded pile of mosquito nets. Cases of food, boxes of cold drinks and medical supplies filled the narrow cabin below.

Soon one of the rangers called to the helmsman to alter course and the big launch headed towards the destination which he knew lay beyond a curtain of waterlogged trees. The little boats behind swung out in an arc, tossing against the swell; then, as the launch settled on a straight course, came into line again. The helmsman throttled down, and the boats threaded slowly through the trees. A man leaned over the prow of the launch, warning of rocks, or jagged stumps of trees ahead. The engine cut back more, barely turning the screw which sometimes brushed over branches just beneath the surface. The ropes were cast off the small boats, and they separated, drifting apart and into the floating weed bordering the uncertain shoreline of the island.

At last they grounded on the soft mud lapped by the miniature waves, and the larger craft, deeper of draught than the others, rode moored to a tree, further away from the island's edge. The water was still only waist-high for the line of men who passed the equipment from hand to hand, then on to the others who stood only ankle-deep on the muddy shore.

The rolls of nets, the poles and the hammers, and all the gear were stacked together on dry land; the food, drink and medical supplies were set out neatly on a slab of rock under the thin shade of an acacia tree.

A white man — hardly white, for like the four others of his

kind, he was tanned by the wind and sun to a deep bronze —
waded ashore from the big launch. He was so tall, the water
reached only to his hips, and the high-crowned bush hat he
wore made him tower above all his companions. Though he
was sparsely built, with lean features, he was immensely
strong. The Matabele in the team which had worked with him
since the beginning of the flood, had named him Ijongojongo,
'the man who grows to the sky', and their deep respect and
affection for him were not lessened when they addressed him
thus to his face.

He was their leader, of course, the man in charge, and
before his sodden suede boots touched dry land he was
issuing orders to those of his men already on shore. Without
pausing to speak, he strode off into the thick bush, followed
by two white rangers and four black men, two of them with
rifles slung over their shoulders. There had been no report of
dangerous game on this island, except, perhaps, a few
buffalo, but it was better to take no chances.

Two small herds of impala, a handful of kudu and waterbuck, the aeroplane pilot had said back at the base camp, and
he thought he might have spotted some buffalo under the tree
cover. But no lions, no rhinos nor other heavy stuff; of that he
was pretty sure. It was the same sort of message he'd had on
one other memorable occasion, thought Ijongojongo, when
the report had failed to mention a pair of cantankerous black
rhinos that had taken four days to shift to the mainland. From
this experience, he knew how important it was to check
carefully for the presence of potentially dangerous game, and
remove them out of the way first. Elephants were easily
persuaded to swim away, as a rule. Lions and buffaloes often
left of their own accord as soon as they scented man; leopards
were seldom seen at all.

The reconnaissance of the island took up most of the
morning, although it was less than a couple of square miles in
area. Ijongojongo was satisfied that, this time, the pilot had
been reasonably correct in his assessment; there were no
heavyweights, not even a buffalo, and only four kudus which
he knew would take to the water without much persuasion.

The main task, then, was to trap and remove to the permanent mainland the impalas, warthogs, baboons, monkeys, bushbuck and any other small creatures they could find. But this would not be immediately. They had come across one herd of impalas in a glade, over on the other side of the island near its narrowest width, but had not disturbed them. It was a small herd of about twenty head, with four or five full-grown rams and a young one, barely a year old. They all looked, from a distance, in fair condition, though probably weakened enough with lack of food to make capture easy. Ijongojongo's eyes were drawn to the largest of the males, an exceptionally fine specimen despite his under-nourished ap-pearance, standing a little apart from the others. It is always diffi-cult to recognise indi-vidual wild animals, especially from a dis-tance, and none of the men carried binoculars; but Ijongojongo was sure in his own mind that he had seen this one before. That the ram remembered him was unlikely; yet he had  a strong feeling this could be so, for the impala was staring in his direction, quite motionless, and he would not have been surprised had he walked towards him in animal greeting. He shrugged off the fantasy, and turned with the others, re-treating into the bush to resume the survey of the island.

They found it to be shaped, roughly, as a figure of eight, and down at the bottom end of it they encountered more impalas. Like the first herd they had seen, all showed the unmistakable signs of approaching poor condition; hind-quarters angular, and the ribs just visible under the skin. But they were quite a long way from actual starvation. It was a larger herd, and Ijongojongo counted over thirty before they leapt away to cover, startled by a sound neither he nor his men could hear.

The team of men camped near the shore just below the narrow waist of the island. It was a week before they began preparations to capture the bulk of the island's inhabitants. Meanwhile, two of the kudus left, swimming easily away to the mainland, little more than a mile distant, with one of the small boats escorting them in case help were needed. Several antbears were flushed out of their holes, trussed up with ropes, carried to the camp and temporarily caged. Similarly dealt with was a fierce little honey-badger, though he was not tied with rope, but wrapped in a net before being released into his cage. Young vervet monkeys and baboons were caught, a few mongooses and nightapes, a pair of porcupines, and a solitary warthog which was dug out of a hole. These, and many others, were taken away from the island in the small boats, and released on the mainland shoreline.

Only then, when most of the remaining animals were warthogs, impalas and smaller antelope, were nets, shovels, stakes, hammers and nylon stockings carried from the camp to the narrowest width of the island, where the trap was to be set.

The nine-foot-high net at the far end of the trap was secured to trees and poles, forming a broad half-circle across the island's waist, from shore to shore; it was pegged down at the base. Another net, the 'gate' into the enclosure, was carefully rolled and laid along a shallow ditch. At each end of the gate, ropes were looped over sturdy branches so that it could be hoisted quickly to close the trap. Every trace of the trench hiding the net was covered with soil and leaves, so that the animals would not suspect the earth had been disturbed.

At each extremity of the gate, two black men crouched, up to their knees in water. The vet sat with one pair, Ijongojongo with the other. Hidden among bushes at strategic points at each end of the raised trap net, two groups of eight black men, with a game ranger to each group, squatted down and waited for the drive to begin, from the far end of the island.

Twenty-four men, with the remaining ranger, had meanwhile taken the three small boats to the island's extremity, disembarked, and after cutting off long, twiggy sticks from the trees, spread out and started advancing through the bush, thick and woody in places, but sometimes open, though rocky and rough underfoot. They began the drive quietly, getting used to the terrain, slowly working up their excitement as a few animals were disturbed, running or leaping before them towards the trap, zigzagging in panic, particularly the warthogs, whose bulky bodies crashed through the dry thickets, snapping off branches, sounding like staccato bursts of rifle fire. One huge hog suddenly turned in a flurry of flying dust and stones; he charged, his coarse hair bristling, warty head lowered with the curved, vicious tusks weaving from side to side, ready to slice into man-flesh. At this challenge, the men's silence was broken — the hunt was on, and with cries of "ahoia — oola, waiee, waiee!" those threatened by the warthog ran, and flayed the ground with their sticks. All along the line the shouts were taken up, everyone running as fast as he could,

stumbling over rocks, twisting and turning between the trees. The brave warthog's courage failed; he dug in his hooves, turned and ran off towards the trap.

The shouts and the sound of the beating lifted a frightened flock of marabou storks out of the trees; they croaked their guttural calls, annoyed at losing a feast of carrion as the animals starved to death, and they flew off to a more peaceful hunting-ground.

A herd of impalas suddenly broke from cover near the water's edge, running, closely packed at first, across and in front of the beaters. Then, as they leapt in panic towards the opposite shore, seeing water again, they doubled back, but turned away from the running men, spreading out, heading in the direction of the trap.

It was a stampede now — impalas, warthogs, bushbuck, duikers and grysbok, baboons and monkeys running with them — all fleeing towards the net hidden under the soil, quite close now. The remaining kudus, and a small group of waterbuck had already slipped away and taken to the water, swimming away, escorted by one of the small boats which circled around them on the look-out for stragglers, the crew ready, if necessary, to rope and tow them to safety.

Most of the panic-stricken animals had crossed the unseen gate-net when Ijongojongo, who still crouched with the two men at one end of it, saw another herd of impalas calmly walking out of a thicket just ahead of the line beaters. Two or three of them made as if to run from the shouting men, but after a few tentative, forward lopes, they resumed their walking. As they approached, close to where he was, not crouching now, but half-standing in astonishment, he counted them. There were seventeen does, a young ram with six-inch horns, and five full-grown rams; they were the ones he had seen several days ago, in the glade.

He was certain there had been another time, in another place, when he had seen the leading ram before; he was sure the impala looked at him as he passed by and crossed the buried net, as though in unmistakable recognition. He thought he saw, shining dully in the dappled sunlight filtering through the tree cover, a metal tag on one of the ram's ears, but could not be sure if any others were also tagged.

Then it was all pandemonium once more, and he turned his mind to other matters. Some of the impalas who had entered the enclosure first had tried to leap the main net, but

failed, becoming entangled. Men rushed in to extricate them, braving the slashing hooves and whipping horns. Those who were not caught up in the net ran to either side, hoping to reach the water, but even there the net still confronted them. More doubled back, some leaping over the gate as it was being raised, escaping through the line of beaters which had contracted to the narrow width of the island's waist. A few of the smaller antelope managed to charge straight through the main net and got away; warthogs threw their great weight against it and the rope was torn apart as they hurtled through.

The gate was up, and all the available men pitched in to the enclosure to deal with the milling crowd of terrified animals, who could not understand that the men were there to help them; most, if not all, soon to begin a new life in places where, the men knew, the floodwaters would never reach. Everything was still confusion. The animals continued to throw themselves about, impalas leaping and plunging, pulling back from the imprisoning net wall, and the warthogs who had not succeeded in breaking through charged at anything that moved, man or beast. Adding to the noise, a shot was fired now and then to put some badly injured animal out of its pain, if it could not be saved by the vet. Shock acted quickly with some, and they died before treatment could be given; shock seemed to be communicated through the larger herd of impalas, for nearly half of them died even before they had been rounded up.

But with the smaller herd of twenty-three, it was a different story. Before Ijongojongo entered the enclosure to take command, he had watched the herd closely for a few moments. Never, during all his many years in the bush, had he witnessed such extraordinary behaviour from a bunch of impalas, or any wild animals, for that matter. Certainly not in the last ten months since the Zambezi river had flooded to unprecedented heights after the dam wall had been closed. It was astounding, beyond comprehension, that a herd, small as it was, which could not have had any more contact with humans than thousands of others — probably unfavourable, at that — had walked calmly into the traumatic situation of

other, terrorised animals, and shouting, running men, as
though they were as tame and domesticated as a herd of farm
cattle. They came up to the net which bulged and shook
violently as other creatures tore into it, or through it, and
stood motionless except for heads turning, seeming to watch
the wild activity going on with interest, almost, Ijongojongo
would have said, with disdain.

With an effort, he took his eyes and mind off them, to
cope with more pressing problems. Gradually, things began
to quieten down. The smaller animals — monkeys, mongooses,
young baboons and bushbabies — were dropped into sacks.
Larger ones, and the survivors of the first impala herd, had
their legs tied with plaited nylon stockings, used in preference
to rope as they were elastic and did not chafe. It was no use
tying warthogs or antbears with nylon; they were bound
securely with strong rope, warthog snouts anchored to flat
pieces of wood to prevent them wounding the men or fellow-
creatures.

All those trussed up were laid in heavy shade, and while
they awaited their turn to be carried to the boats, they were
splashed with water to keep body temperatures down,
helping to restore normal breathing and heartbeats.

As some men dismantled the nets, others carried the
animals the short distance to the boats at the shore. They
moved in single file except when four worked together to
carry warthogs or antbears, wrapped in netting and slung
between poles. It was a slow, lengthy process, for the men
were tired and hot after their efforts and the excitement of the
drive and capture. The number of animals seemed endless.

While these activities were going on, and the vet was kept
busy attending to the many slight injuries, both human and
animal, Ijongojongo with another game ranger walked over to
the group of impalas which remained standing, mostly, to one
side of where the net had been. As they approached, slowly
and enticingly, careful to make no sudden movement, none of
the impalas took fright, except three or four who backed away
a little nervously, defecating as they did so. The dominant
male actually came forward, head up and horns held high, and

as Ijongojongo and his companion stopped, the ram stopped
too, not three paces away. And there, the men saw clearly,
was a tag clipped to his left ear. It was one of theirs, both men
agreed. Then Ijongojongo remembered; but Kali-Anuka had
known before.

12

WHEN, in the glade, the Pambuka herd had stiffened at the presence of the Zimikile, Kali-Anuka stood very still, sniffed at the air and caught every sound made by the intruders. There was a faint familiarity regarding one in particular, when a Zimikile spoke so low, not imagining the impala ram would hear. But Kali-Anuka did hear, without understanding, and he was sure it was the same voice he had heard after he had been lifted out of the river and laid exhausted on the floating carrier. He strained his eyes towards the group of men whose heads showed above the barrier of bushes, but they were too far away for any to be recognisable. But he was sure; he heard the voice and he saw, though blurred, the wide, tall hat which no other had worn that day on the river.

He felt the urge to approach this Zimikile, not to confirm beyond doubt his identity, but to prove to himself, once and for all, that the man meant no harm, only the kindness which had shown in his face on the carrier, and again in the vision which had come to him, when the man had spoken in a language he had understood. He started forward, but caught a glimpse of what looked like a Zimikile stick held by another, and he was filled with the old, rooted animal distrust, and thought of Mwami.

The men backed away, and were gone, treading noisily on the dry sticks and leaves as they walked away. They *must* be trusted, thought Kali-Anuka, and argued with himself yet again. But this time it was a one-sided argument, and positive. All the evidence he had stored in his memory — almost all of it — pointed to trust. The zebras Tantalika had seen, saved from drowning or starvation; his own experience, plucked from the moment of death in the river; Teketa and most of his party taken off the other island, and then the seven does. There was one thing common to all these events — a tall, thin Zimikile, wearing a strange covering for his head; and he had come again. Kali-Anuka had not forgotten the other things, the tales Mwami had told, Mwami's own horrible death, the great man-mountain across the river, and the flood. But these were, surely,nothing to do with the tall Zimikile or any of those in his herd. And there was something else. For the first time since the incident with the wild dog, he recalled meeting Kwizima, the impala from the north. How had he and his herd crossed the river? Was this, too, the work of the Zimikile?

He called softly to his impalas, and they came to gather loosely around their leader.

"Listen," he said in a voice loud enough for all to hear, "listen to what I have to tell you. It's important that every one of you — you too, Mwami-Mupati," he added as his young son wandered off to a little tuft of grass which no one else had seen, "do as I say, without question."

He paused for a moment, as they all closed in towards him.

"I'm sure the Zimikile have come to help us, and it will

help them if we show no fear. From what Teketa and the others have told us, it seems as though we and all the animals here will be driven to the floating carriers, and carried away to some other place."

"But it may be for something worse!" interrupted one of the does, but this time it was not Silulimi.

"I don't think that's possible, do you? Nothing can be worse than living here, and we cannot go on our own. Let these Zimikile do what they will, and we cannot be in more of a fix than we are now."

"They have come to kill us, perhaps to put us out of our misery!" wailed Silulimi.

"No, Silulimi, my dear," Kali-Anuka said soothingly. "If that is their intention, it would have happened already. But they will surely do that," he went on, "if we panic, as some did before, and break a leg or a neck, or leap into the water, unable to swim. Keep calm, whatever you do, and follow my example all the time."

"And what will that be, Kali-Anuka?" asked Teketa.

"I will do what I think the Zimikile will want me to do — not what they will expect of me."

There was a quiet, impala hubbub of conversation while Swilila and Kusomona came closer to Kali-Anuka, to nuzzle and lick him with affection.

"That was perfect, Kali, everything you said," murmured Swilila, "and if the others feel as I do, they are comforted, and will do exactly what you have said."

"I think I could even get to like the Zimikile," Kusomona said, her tongue licking close to his ear.

"Some are good — they must be," he said firmly, but almost to himself. Then: "Whatever happens, Kusomona, you must keep Mupati near to you, for although he's almost old enough to look after himself, we mustn't let anything happen to him. He, more than any of us, mustn't be allowed to panic."

She licked him again.

"Don't worry — I'll see to him," she whispered.

During the dry days that followed they knew the Zimikile

were active on the island, and sometimes, through a break in
the trees, they saw them moving about. Once, on the far side
of the glade, they watched as a group of men worked at
widening the entrance to an antbear's hole, then digging deep
into the hard ground to bring out a female and her baby.
There was a long, dusty struggle with the mother, but
eventually she was subdued with the aid of a net, which to the
impalas resembled a squarely woven, giant spider's web, the
strands as thick as their own legs. Secured, the bundle of
antbear was carried away, slung between two poles, and the
furry baby was cradled in the tall Zimikile's arms.

Every day the impalas heard them, the sounds coming
from different parts of the island, shouting and calling; on
three occasions there was the sharp bang from one of their
sticks, and even Kali-Anuka flinched as the others ran a short
distance in alarm. He began to wonder, as the days passed, if
the Zimikile would ever come near the herd again, and he
listened all the time for the tell-tale sound of the floating
carrier-creatures to roar into noisy life and go away from the
island, leaving them to their inevitable fate. Several times his
heart sank when the sound came, but it lasted only briefly,
dying away with a spluttering burst, and he knew the Zimikile
had not left.

One morning, he had led the herd down to the edge of the
lake, where pools of shallow water had collected, easy to
reach. There was a lot of activity going on across the
narrowest part of the island, through the trees and bush not
far away from where they drank. Later, from the opposite
direction, there were shouts and the crashing of undergrowth.
The impalas stopped drinking, raised their heads and turned
their ears to the sounds.

Teketa, close enough to Kali-Anuka to be heard, spoke
quietly.

"It is the same as they did on the other island," he said.
"Look — they cannot be far away."

Through the gaps in the trees they saw other animals
running in terror. Streaks of brown and white — the other
impalas — hurtled by, disappearing quickly into the depths of
the bush beyond.

Kali-Anuka moved among his herd.

"Come," he said to them as he brushed by each one. "Come— follow me, and remember that we do not run, or leap like those others. Think that you are going to a place where there will be plenty of fresh green leaves to eat, and tender roots and grasses; where we will have no enemies, no sickness. Think only of those things — and do as I do."

Head held high, carrying his horns as proudly as a king carries his crown, he marched off at a steady pace towards salvation, or to the long silence of death — he knew not which, for certain. And the others followed.

Kali-Anuka looked up at the tall Zimikile, and wished he could make him understand what he wanted to say. Had there been any possibility of that, he would have begun with a question.

"Do you remember me, Zimikile?" he would have asked. "You once saved my life, and seemed glad that you had."

But there was no need for words, for there was the same look on the Zimikile's long, lean face he had seen before. The eyes crinkled and the mouth widened; he was recognised, and the Zimikile was grateful he still lived.

Ijongojongo bent his head, and slowly lifted an outstretched hand towards the impala. He said to himself, as so many men had said before — as he had thought a hundred, a thousand times — if only animals could talk, how much better the world would be, how much more we would understand!

The impala came to him, lowering his muzzle to lick the palm of his hand with his rough, curled tongue, and Ijongojongo carefully stretched his other hand to stroke the soft neck. The ranger beside him, astonished, dared not move, not wanting to break the spell, this moment of magic. Nor could he believe the evidence of his own eyes.

There was no doubt about it, they both decided in whispered undertones — this thin, undernourished ram was the same one they had, between them, pulled out of the water in the earliest days of the flooding. It was, if they strained their credulity to its limits, acceptable that this impala remembered, and understood that he owed his life to them. But no matter how they tried, they could not accept that the ram had been able to communicate to all the twenty-two impalas of his herd, that men need not be feared, that they had come to save and not to destroy.

Ijongojongo tried something else, moving in slow-motion to reach up and break off two handfuls of leaves; then he offered them to the ram and two does who had come closer. They grasped at them eagerly, and he signalled to his companion to do the same. For some time the two men were kept busy handing the leaf clusters down, and none of the impalas showed the slightest sign of nervousness. It was as though they had all been bred in captivity, with no more fear of men than pampered domestic pets. It was nothing less than uncanny, thought Ijongojongo, and no one else would ever believe such a thing except those of his team who were actually witnessing all that was transpiring, standing back open-mouthed, their work forgotten.

There was more to come. As Ijongojongo turned away to order the men, good-naturedly, to get on with rolling up the dismantled netting, the impala ram followed him with the others close behind. So he went on walking, and there was no need to tie their legs and have them carried to the shore — they were content to walk there of their own accord.

There was a great gathering of animals near the shore, where the small ones wriggled in sacks, and mounds of warthogs and antbears, legs and snouts bound with rope, rolled and twisted ineffectually. Impalas and other antelopes lay on the ground, front and back legs tied securely together, for there is a special way to carry ruminants to prevent internal damage. Kali-Anuka and the Pambuka did not entirely escape having their legs tied after they had reached the holding point near the anchored boats; they did not understand why it was necessary, but submitted without resistance.

The afternoon sun was far advanced when the last animal, a porcupine, with quills sticking out of his sack, was brought down from the netting zone, and dumped with all the others. A team of men under a game ranger had meanwhile tagged ears, noted details including sex, weight and estimated age, for recognition and scientific study at a later stage.

The small boats were loaded first; then, because Ijongojongo regarded them as deserving special treatment, all the impalas of Kali-Anuka's herd were carried the short distance through waist-high water to the big launch, and laid tenderly on the aft deck under the awning. The journey did not take long. They came in under a range of yellow hills, following the course of a river which had doubled its width in the last ten months, flowing south. It was hardly recognisable as a river, for it was covered with a green floating weed which had flourished in the calm waters of the growing lake, spreading rapidly. The boats advanced slowly, hardly moving through the layer of weed, and several times the engine of the big boat was stopped, while the propeller was freed of its entanglements.

Before sunset, the flotilla drifted in to a treeless shoreline, and the men hurried to discharge their cargoes before the mosquitoes descended on them, hungry for blood. One by one, from each boat, the animals were lifted out and carried to the wide stretch of open ground which rose steeply up to the hills beyond. In groups of a kind, or singly with those likely to turn on their rescuers — as the warthogs did frequently — their bonds were cut, or untied. Mostly, they raced off as fast as they could, eager to reach the cover of the trees growing on the side of the hills; and the men called words of good luck to them as they went.

The last to be freed were the impalas, those of the Pambuka herd first. Ijongojongo, alone, untied the legs of Kali-Anuka, and wondered if his behaviour would be any different after the ordeal. He was not disappointed. The ram struggled to his hooves, and stood calmly watching the activities going on around him. As his own impalas were freed from the nylon bonds, he moved to each in turn, nuzzling and licking them. If he had not known better, Ijongojongo would have sworn he heard strange word-sounds issuing from the ram's mouth.

When the last was freed, they all stood in a group with their leader, not running off, as though waiting for his instructions. But Kali-Anuka gave none; he was too preoccupied observing the other herd as they were brought to the shore and, like themselves, untied. The dominant male was the first to scramble to his hooves, but he did not run off; he walked over to Kali-Anuka and gave a little bow of submission, and the other leader understood the significance of it. Then Kwizima — for it was indeed he — approached each member of his clan as they lay on the ground, and lowered his mouth to their ears. When they all stood, some shaking a little with an inward fear, he led them back to where Kali-Anuka awaited them.

The men on the shore, those still standing in the water, and the others on the boats, all watched this extraordinary display in utter astonishment, the black men more incredulous than the white. Their wonderment became disbelief when the two leader rams walked up to Ijongojongo, as though they had both known and trusted him all their lives, and nuzzled against his bare chest. He fondled them behind their tagged ears, and the watchers stared, spellbound, as the combined impala herd turned at an unheard order from Kali-Anuka, and leapt away across the open ground. They moved easily, their hooves barely touching the ground as they glided away in long leaps towards the edge of the woodland slopes. A cloud of dust, golden from the setting sun, rose like a transparent curtain over the line of trees, and the men on the shore and on the boats stood motionless in a great and marvellous silence.

Certainly, the events of this day were to be told and retold in many a tribesman's kraal throughout the land, and the tale is enshrined in African legend. And certainly, one white man — the tall, thin one they called Ijongojongo, held this memory in his mind and in his heart, for as long as he lived.

13

CONCEALED among the tangled bushes on the edge of a little creek which curved sharply off the southward course of the tributary, a solitary black heron waited for the sun to rise high enough to heat the surface of the water, bringing the fish within reach of his beak, below the floating weed. When he judged the time was right, he stepped daintily into the water, stirring the weed to expose little pools, and stretched out his wings to make a shady canopy so that he could see his prey more clearly.

Nearby, as the sun burnt the early morning mist away, a chameleon, still as a fossil, gripped on to a small branch of a waterlogged wild pear tree, heavy with fruit, although it was slowly dying. The chameleon's tongue, as long as its pale green body, flicked invisibly to catch a bright-winged butterfly which had settled on a dark fruit; then it was washed down with dew lapped from a leaf.

A small flock of long-legged sandpipers thrust their thin, pointed beaks at the weed, snapping up insect larvae. Suddenly startled by the splash of a big fish, or an otter, across the water, they took to the air, voicing their alarm with a chorus of whistled 'tchicks'. They circled, still twittering, then quickly returned to their feeding-ground.

It was peaceful here, and although the early rains had begun, the level of the water had not risen since Kali-Anuka had chosen this place, and the territory around it, as his new home range.

There was an abundant variety of vegetation, some new to the herd, but mostly palatable. Many of the trees they had been familiar with in the past grew here, but there were fewer mopanes and acacias. They ate off the jesse bush, bush-willows and, when in reach, browsed the leaves of shepherd's trees. At this time the waxy-white flowers of baobabs were falling, and soon there would be the slender, yellow acorns from the crocodile-bark trees to chew. They had found, to their delight, the sweet grass of their old haunt growing close to the edge of the creek; they would be assured of food, all year round.

Later that morning they came down to the creek, and stood on the grassy edge, few of them drinking, for with the first rain showers they had taken all the moisture they needed from the grass and leaves.

The Pambuka herd numbered nearly forty head now, since the others had joined them. After hearing Kwizima's story of how he had brought his herd, with great courage and wisdom, across the river before it had flooded, Kali-Anuka welcomed him and the survivors of his clan to integrate with the Pambuka, and Kwizima was appointed second-in-command. He had submitted to Kali-Anuka's dominance without question; he was hardly in a position to challenge the Pambuka leader's authority, nor did he wish to.

Already there had been a number of casualties, mostly among the old and the weak; but it was no more than could be expected in such a vast area, teeming with animals, many brought in the Zimikile boats, with many carnivorous predators among them. Seventeen does were pregnant; Kusomona was with lamb again, but neither her mother nor Swilila had conceived at the time of the last breeding season.

So, as Kali-Anuka munched grass at the creek, with Kusomona at his side, he felt well content. The flooding had ceased, and even if it should come again there were the hills, and the high escarpment behind them open for escape.

He was about to lift his mouth from the grass, when a dark shape erupted from the thick layer of weed which lay over the water nearby. The impalas jumped back in alarm; others behind and to either side of them turned, poised ready to run. The sandpipers took off, 'tchick-tchicking' away in flight, and the chameleon changed colour.

"Wa buka?" squeaked Tantalika, and stood with his head above the weed, his dark eyes sparkling a greeting.

"I am well — and all the better for seeing you, Tantalika!" answered Kali-Anuka, all thought of an unpleasant death by a crocodile dispelled.

"Oh, Tantalika — we're so pleased you've come!" Kusomona agreed. "How did you find us?"

"Fura-Uswa told me where you had been taken by the Zimikile. As soon as we knew, we came, and settled in a splendid holt under some rocks quite close by. There are no crabs or mussels there, but the river's full of fish."

"And Vutuka?" asked Kusomona. "Is she . . . ? Has she . . . ?"

The otter's teeth chattered gaily, and he held up three fingers.

"All males," he said, "and all swimming fine."

At once, there was another eruption of the weed, and four heads popped above the surface. One of them belonged to Vutuka, who shrieked with joy, and in a moment all were rushing about in great excitement, nipping at the impalas' legs with their sharp little teeth.

Later, in the heat of the day, while the three young cubs slept curled together close to their mother, Kali-Anuka told the parent otters of the events which had led to the enlarged Pambuka herd coming to its new habitat, and although he could not compete with the impala's story, Tantalika related his own.

They grouped themselves under the shade of two stocky shepherd's trees — the otters, Kali-Anuka and Kusomona, Swilila, Silulimi and Yandika. It was just like the long-gone days, all being together again.

"While Vutuka and I were seeking another new home," said Tantalika, "Fura-Uswa called me to him in a dark cave, high in the side of a mountain," — he pointed to the escarpment which rose sharply away to the west — "and when I got there he told me many things. But the most important was that this mountain, the land below and around it would never be flooded, that this was the place where many animals would be brought by the Zimikile; they would live in normal animal peace for many, many moons. He no longer seemed angry with the Zimikile — he seemed almost pleased with what they were doing. 'There will no longer be need,' he said, 'for you to watch over impalas, for they will be protected by the Zimikile.'

"He said he was tired, and wished to rest his spirit. This would come, he said, when rhinoceros of his kind return to the Great Valley, which would be quite soon. I could not doubt him, for he knows everything!

"He sent greetings to you, Kali-Anuka, and when I told him I might not be able to find you again, he laughed — I had never heard him laugh before, and it was quite frightening!"

Silulimi tapped a hoof impatiently.

"Oh, do go on, Tantalika!"

"He laughed, as I said," continued the otter, "and then in that funny voice of his, he squeaked, 'Go where I have told you many animals will go, and you will find him!' "

"And why did it take you so long?" asked Kali-Anuka.

Tantalika looked down at the three cubs, still sleeping, and there was no need for a reply.

The heat was oppressive, and there was a distant roll of thunder from the north. Vutuka had already joined her cubs in sleep, and Tantalika's head began to droop, his eyes fluttering with fatigue. His head jerked up as he thought of something else the impalas should know.

"Nyaminyami, the godkin known to the black Zimikile, is still very angry, and his spirit is restless." Tantalika yawned widely. "He has vowed that one day..." his head lolled across Vutuka's neck, and his eyes closed completely for a moment, "... one day the valley will be freed of the waters covering it. They will press down on the Zimikile's dam until..." it was all he could do to get the words out, "... until it breaks, and is swept away ..."

His eyes closed again, and with his chin resting on Vutuka's neck, he began to snore.

EPILOGUE

FROM the moment when the flow of the Zambezi river was blocked by the sealing of the last gaps in the Kariba dam wall, four and a half years passed before the lake reached its full capacity, in May 1963. Since then, give or take a few feet, the level has remained constant, and unless Nyaminyami carries out his pledge to free the river from its bondage, it will remain constant for as long as man can foresee the future.

The Great Valley is at peace now; the deep wound which man inflicted is healing, for he has come to terms with Nature, and Nature, perhaps, with him. Both are receiving the benefits from the forming of the lake. For man there is the hydro-electric power for his homes and industries in Zimbabwe and in Zambia, with a vast playground for his leisure, where he can gain new knowledge of Nature's ways.

For Nature there is a sanctuary for all her children of the Great Valley in the areas which border the lake, and there is the lake itself.

In one area, where the sweet grass, so beloved by the Pambuka herd of impalas, grows again along a curving beach, the descendants of Kali-Anuka are thriving.

You may, should you journey to Kariba, come across the impalas in some Utopian glade, close to the lake shore; do not expect them to approach you, trustingly, as Kali-Anuka and the others approached Ijongojongo, long ago. For the words of Kali-Anuka are remembered by the Pambuka herd, and all the impalas in the Great Valley.

"There are good and bad Zimikile," he had often said, "and I am never able to tell the difference."

Perhaps he knows now, and Tantalika, too, for neither of them still roams through the wild Zambezi Valley.

Nor does Ijongojongo.

END